Strings Attached

PALMETTO
PUBLISHING
Charleston, SC
www.PalmettoPublishing.com

Hardcover ISBN: 9798822973831
Paperback ISBN: 9798822973848
eBook ISBN: 9798822973855

Strings Attached

by
Andrew Nitkin

Contents

FIRST MOVEMENT:
EUROPE

CHAPTER 1

The Invitation

The view of the Hudson River had always been breathtaking from my 35th floor apartment in New York City. As I stood by my window entranced, I wondered how it all happened. How and why did I get involved with a scheme so dark and sinister it almost ruined the career I'd worked so hard to build. Building a career as a concert guitarist is not for the faint of heart; it took years of practice to perfect technique and interpretation, as well as handling all that goes into a career business-wise, almost all down the drain due to one bad decision I made five years ago. That fateful decision changed my life forever.

It all started when I was contracted in the winter of 2018 to do a five-city tour of Europe by the European Union Cultural Council that would start in the fall of 2018. They called my manager Jeanine and requested my availability. I had been invited to Spain a few months earlier to judge the Andres Segovia Guitar Competition and had given a short recital at the United States Embassy for invited guests that was well received by the dignitaries that attended. Jeanine informed me that Juan Carlos Garcia, the Spanish representative from the consulate who attended had recommended me for the tour. He was a well-educated, well-dressed Spaniard who appreciated the arts and especially the Spanish guitar, as it's called, which originated in Spain centuries ago. Juan Carlos would play a pivotal part in what transpired in Spain. He had an air about him that I couldn't quite identify.

I conferred with my wife, Eve, saying "This would be great for my career to take it to the next level. I haven't accepted the offer yet, but it pays extremely well and I will be away from home for a minimum of four weeks." Eve responded, "I hope you are right about this and it's not a wasted trip. If you feel strongly about it, I'm onboard." I called and told Juan Carlos I would accept the offer, and he responded "Great, I will let the council know and we can go ahead with the arrangements for it."

Eve, an intelligent, tall, beautiful redhead with whom I fell in love with fifteen years ago, was used to this sort of thing as a professional woman, but usually I would only be gone for two weeks or so because of my commitment to my teaching job at Manhattan University. Having built the guitar department there single-handedly, it was hard to get away for an extended period of time unless I could provide good reason to the university. This tour would help promote the guitar department there so I knew they would happily agree to it. Also, more recently, I had been turning my duties over to my assistant, Andrew Sisley, who would take over in my absence. Andrew was a former student of mine and someone I had one hundred percent trust in to run a tight ship so I felt confident I could accept the tour without worrying about things back home.

My program, which I sent into the Council, was listed as Jonathan Lanbourne, Classical Guitarist, and would consist of the following repertoire:

Suite Espanola by Gaspar Sanz

Chaconne in D by Johann Sebastian Bach

Two pieces (Asturias, Torre Bermeja) by Isaac Albeniz

Two preludes (Numbers 2 & 5) by Heitor Villa-Lobos

Two Improvisations – Malaguena, Rumba (in the style of)

Other pieces subject to addition. Two guitars would be used for the performances*

*Pedro de Miguel from Spain, flamenco guitar with spruce top and Indian Rosewood sides and back, to be used for all Spanish and general Latin repertoire,

*Armin Hanika from Germany, classical guitar with spruce top and Mexican Palo Escrito wood sides and back, to be used for Bach and more modern classical repertoire.

Having worked on this repertoire for months and years, I was confident I was ready to perform it well. I was ready to take my career to the next level and become an international star like my idol, Andres Segovia, and walk in his footsteps. Years of hard work had prepared me for this. The tour would start in London, then go on to Brussels, Paris, Rome, and finally Madrid. There would be one to two concert recitals in each city depending on the venues booked. All of my travel and expenses would be handled by the travel agency that worked with the European Union Cultural Council, so I felt I was in good hands. Little did I know what was planned for me once I got to Madrid. The fact that I survived it all was a miracle, but it changed me forever. The life of a concert musician should be simple—show up and perform to the best of your ability. Draw in the audience and entertain, but also profoundly touch them. What happened otherwise fell completely out of that world. A different reality completely, as I found out and was forced to endure. My world was simple, the world of espionage was complicated and full of obstacles.

Growing up in a small town in New Jersey, I felt I had done about all I could in New York City, so this tour came at an opportune time. I needed artistically to get out to other countries and show what I had to offer the classical guitar music world. The ensuing months from the winter of 2018 to the start of the tour in Fall of 2018 were spent preparing for it. Heavy practice sessions paired with work on the logistics of the tour that I prepared with Jeanine took up most of my time as well as making sure things would be taken care of at home. Jeanine for some reason would extend our meetings beyond what was needed. I felt that was nice of her. She also was someone who had an air to her I couldn't completely identify.

The life of a concert guitarist or for that matter any accomplished instrumentalist in the classical world doesn't come easily. The competition is fierce for a limited amount of available work and so much goes into it. Not only many hours and years of practice and preparation but also developing the business side of it that includes developing an image that can be marketed and sold. To have a sustainable concert career, there must be return engagements for years as well as new venues sought out. To be successful, one must aggressively pursue it every day. It was something I've always wanted, and I just needed the right break to present itself. I hoped this was it.

When September 2018 rolled around, I was ready to go. My flight would leave JFK airport at 8pm on September 15th and was due to arrive the following morning at Heathrow Airport with transport to the Royal Hotel in London. As the plane departed, I was hyped up for the tour and ready to take the European classical music world by storm. My first performance would be for the Classical Guitar Society at a university in London on September 20th with the more important performance being at Wigmore Hall on September 22nd, a perfect size venue for the guitar. I was following in the footsteps of the great guitarists who had performed there, Segovia, Bream, Williams, etc.... and it felt great! I would add my name to music history as an American and use it as a steppingstone to more opportunities.

CHAPTER 2

London

As the plane descended into Heathrow I was struck by the beauty of London in the air. Westminster Abby, Big Ben, London Bridge, and more were all visible from the air on a clear day. When I got through customs a car was there waiting to take me to the Royal Hotel in the heart of London. I checked into the hotel, took a short nap, and then hit the streets to familiarize myself with the area. It was around lunchtime, so I grabbed a bite to eat in one of the pubs nearby that the English are famous for. Fish and chips with Oxford Rye Whiskey made for a very enjoyable lunch.

John Anderson was my European Council contact in London, and we met for dinner that night to discuss London logistics and the itinerary for the tour. John was a typical Englishman, very proper and well spoken, conservatively dressed with greying hair. Of course, who knew what lie beneath? He said, "Jon, you don't mind if I call you Jon, do you? Feel free to do the same." I nodded. All seemed to go well until John warned me, "there might be a minor detour in Spain that you are unaware of. Some sort of recital at a castle outside of Segovia, Spain. I'll have more details for you before you leave for Brussels after your Wigmore Hall debut." I replied "That sounds great, I'm intrigued by it. A castle in Spain! Please get those details to me as soon as possible since they were not in my original itinerary, and I want to be prepared." A castle in Spain? That could be a blast! Little did I know what awaited me there.

The next day I went over to the university to meet with the head of the guitar department, Albert Feeley, who had planned my guitar society recital coming up. He was a very jovial Irish-Englishman who had been in his position for over thirty years. It was a nice visit, and I told him I was ready to perform for them and looked forward to the recital on Thursday. He said we should grab a beer and talk afterwards at a local pub. I said I'd love that and so planned to. This was my chance to find out more about the classical guitar world in England and Europe. Albert was very talkative so I knew it would be an interesting conversation that would give me a good picture of the music scene there.

My next stop was over to Wigmore Hall to check out the hall. John accompanied me there since the press would attend this concert to review my performance. I loved the hall and the history behind it with so many great performers having played there. John then informed me that we had a dinner planned that night with Juan Carlos Garcia who was in town to see my Wigmore Hall debut. I said I would be delighted to see him again so I could thank him for recommending me for the tour. John said he would confirm with Juan Carlos and get back to me. I went back to the hotel and rested a bit and looked forward to dinner and what lay ahead.

We had dinner at the Royal Hotel, whose five-star restaurant was one of the best in London. Juan Carlos was late to show up of course, in keeping with Spanish tradition, but once there, was very charming and welcoming. I found him intriguing and wondered what other areas of business he was involved with outside of the consulate and council. He seemed to have his hands in many projects as he alluded to and, as I was to find out later, Juan Carlos seemed to play his cards close to the vest. I asked him what business he was in and he responded, "I have many different business interests and thanks to family money can play the field in everything, as the American saying goes." I asked him to elaborate but he seemed unwilling, just saying "You will learn more in due time, Jonathan, as we get to know each other better." The food came and went fairly fast; dinner was fabulous of course. During our after-dinner drinks Juan Carlos said, "I will be working with your manager Jeanine and am looking forward to meeting her—let me know when she arrives." I replied "Of course, Jeanine is a very smart, competent manager who you will get along well with." We said our goodbyes after dessert and Juan Carlos said, "I will see you for sure many times to come." I wasn't sure what that meant, but shook it off, not taking it too seriously.

My first performance at the Guitar Society went well but not well enough for me for my upcoming Wigmore Hall debut. I had to step it up a bit to meet my standards. They seemed to love it but my usual nemesis, the Bach *Chaconne*, did not go as well as I would have liked. Wigmore was next and I needed to do better. After drinks and basically interrogating Albert about things, I went back to the room and practiced the Bach some more. Technically, I knew I could handle the *Chaconne*, but interpretively, it was a challenge. J.S. Bach had arrived home after a court commitment that kept him away for months only to find his wife had passed away suddenly due to an illness. The *Chaconne* was part of an unaccompanied violin suite that he wrote around that time. This profound piece of music almost always moves me and brings me to tears. Could I convey that feeling to my audiences on this tour? That was the goal.

On the morning of the 22nd I warmed up my hands, had a full breakfast—I knew I wouldn't be able to eat until after the performance—and took a short early afternoon nap. After waking up refreshed, I was ready to go. I arrived at the hall around 6pm and warmed up onstage. It was awe-inspiring to be there knowing that Wigmore was considered the great small chamber music hall of London, just as Carnegie Hall has the Weil Recital Hall in New York. 8pm rolled around and off I went on stage. The first piece, *Suite Espanola* by Gaspar Sanz, went extremely well. The dance melodies in this piece were used by Joaquin Rodrigo in composing his concerto masterpiece, *Fantasia para un Gentilhombre (Fantasy for a Gentleman)*, so I knew the audience had heard many of these melodies before. The audience response was very encouraging. Next came the Bach *Chaconne*. Again, the profound masterpiece itself that had monumental technical and interpretive challenges. As I played through it, I was inspired by the audience and surroundings and performed the thirteen-minute piece as well as I ever had. I was pleased! After that, the second half of the program's lighter pieces went smoothly and I even had fun with it since, after all, we perform our best when we enjoy it. It ended up being a great night for me and I think for my audience as well! Things just flowed seamlessly.

After the performance, John, Juan Carlos, and Jeanine who had flown in for the debut went out to a late-night dinner. I was pleased and told them how much I looked forward to the following concerts. Next was Brussels, but I had a day to explore London further before leaving. Jeanine said she would stick around and that we could explore together. I was happy she did; I wanted company. Being a 35-year-old single mother, she didn't get away much, so I was happy she could attend, and we got along well. We stopped for drinks at a local bar and Jeanine told me a little about her life, her struggles, and how much she wanted to meet the love of her life. She put her hand on mine at the table and said "Jonathan, I feel very happy tonight being here with you. You have always calmed me down and made me feel safe. I hope we have more evenings like this." I replied, "I'm happy you feel that way." After looking at me intensely, Jeanine then said "It's not easy for me to find a partner who shares my interests and matches up with me well. Our personalities have to be aligned, like you and I are." Being a man, we are sometimes oblivious to signs that women put out. And so it was with

Jeanine that night as well. There would be more to come as I was to find out in many ways.

The next day John confirmed that before going home, I would be adding a recital at a castle in Segovia after my Madrid performance. There would be an extra stipend in it for me, so of course I agreed. I was intrigued to find out who my audience would be at the Castle since it was added last minute. I phoned Eve and told her my trip was extended a bit, so she was aware. She wasn't thrilled, saying she was missing me already and cuddling with me in bed at night, but she understood it was the nature of the business. I told her I missed her too and we would make up for it when I got home. The reviews for the concert were very favorable so I was content with moving on to the next city and on from there.

The next morning, I was up early and ready to go. I caught the Eurostar high speed train at 10am and arrived in Brussels by noon. The first-class accommodations on the train were superb so the trip was very comfortable and going through the tunnel under the English Channel was thrilling. I would be traveling Eurostar to Paris as well, so I looked forward to that. I noticed an odd-looking character on the train with dark glasses and a black suit but didn't think twice about it then. Just took notice of this person for some reason. I would see him again later many times.

Once in Brussels, I took a taxi from the train station to the Grand Palace Hotel in the heart of the city and checked in. Upon arrival, the concierge informed me that I had a message waiting for me that was delivered anonymously.

I thought, "how odd, no name or sender?" I went up to my room, practiced the program again, and rested before going out to meet the mysterious person who sent this message. I thought the lack of an author was a simple oversight on their part. I would find out soon enough.

CHAPTER 3

Brussels

Upon opening the note, the message read "Tonight, Café Brussels, 7pm, don't be late." I was not sure if it was meant for me, so I asked the concierge who delivered it, and he said it came by courier, so it had no name associated with it. I figured I had nothing to lose so I would go. I wasn't checking out the hall at the Conservatoire Royal De Bruxelles until the day after tomorrow so I could stay out a bit tonight. The concert would be on Friday night, September 28th, so I had time to prepare. After walking around the local area for a bit, I went back to the hotel to rest and get ready to go out and meet whoever this person was.

I arrived at Café Brussels at 6:45pm and just stood hidden outside the front door a bit so I could see who was entering the restaurant. At 6:59pm I went in and informed the hostess I was supposed to meet someone here at 7pm but wasn't sure who. She asked me my name and immediately showed me to a table in a private room just off the main dining room. Once I was seated, I heard a woman's voice, "Hi Jonathan, I'm so glad you could make it." As I turned around, I realized I knew the voice—it was Jeanine's.

Jeanine Jones was an extremely smart and capable worker, very well-educated, very beautiful in many ways, and as I had always assumed, lonely. Her previous relationship was with an abusive husband, and I always felt bad for her. She has a good heart. She, a well-endowed blonde, sat down next to me dressed to the hilt, extremely sexy, short skirt, low-cut top, and looking like she was ready for something. I was, of course, taken aback by the whole thing. I asked her why the secrecy and why she was in Brussels. She responded, "Jonathan, I've always been attracted to you, and I think you've felt the same way towards me. I thought this tour was the perfect time to explore our feelings for each other and see if there is anything there. I thought you would not have come tonight if you knew it was me and what I had planned. This was the only way I could get you here without you feeling guilty about meeting me." I thought, "how awkward this is."

Needless to say, I was in a pickle. I needed Jeanine to follow through with the details for the tour, but I was not interested in ruining my marriage for it. I thought maybe complete honesty was the best way to go at this point and I was just hoping for the best. I proceeded to tell Jeanine, "Yes, I am attracted to you and love working with you. But I am not willing to leave my wife with whom I've had a great relationship and have built a life. I appreciate your efforts here tonight but hope you will stay on with me as my manager and friend. I need you as my business manager and nothing more." Jeanine went on to say, "I'm not asking you to leave your wife, just to explore our relationship to see where it could go. I am a very open-minded person." I responded, "I don't think it's a good idea to pursue this and I hope I'm not offending you by saying this." Jeanine went on to say, "I understand Jonathan, maybe you will be more open to something later on, I am a very patient woman and can wait as long as it takes."

Jeanine stood up, bent over and grabbed me and gave me a passionate kiss on the lips. She then said, "Of course Jonathan, I will stay on as your manager. I wouldn't have it any other way. But just think deeply about it. Our relationship could be something very special and fun." She then walked out leaving me with a bottle of wine and some hors d'oeuvres that I felt compelled to consume, alone.

CHAPTER 4
Brussels Continued

When I returned to the hotel around 9pm I went straight to the bar. Whiskey being one of my passions, I ordered a double of Macallan 12 Year Sherry Oak Scotch to help me digest what had just happened. After settling down I went upstairs to my room to rest and figure out how I was going to manage Jeanine and this tour. I decided to just proceed and not make too much of what had happened. It was just a fantasy she had, and if it didn't pan out for her, I hoped she would know that. And the truth is, she was hard to resist, but I knew I would never go there.

The next day I decided to stay in for most of it and practice my program. I had added another piece just in case the audience wanted to hear music that was more modern and dissonant. It was *Invocacion y danza (Invocation and Dance)* by Joaquin Rodrigo, a 20th century Spanish composer. The mystical beginning conjures up visions of indigenous tribal rituals while the ensuing dance segments make it a wonderfully contrasting piece of music to add to the program if necessary. A combination of dissonant and beautiful melodies making for a fascinating audience experience. Being a long, moody piece of music, 15 minutes or so, I would only perform it if the mood and circumstances were right.

After a good day of practice and rest I wandered the area near the hotel after dinner and just enjoyed the shops and cafes of Brussels. Tomorrow I would perform at the Conservatoire Royal de Bruxelles and then take the Eurostar to Paris the next day. I was looking forward to moving on from Brussels. The morning of the concert I received a good luck note with a heart and kiss from Jeanine. She was obviously working on me but since I needed her to execute documents for the tour moving forward, I didn't want to rock the boat, so I just responded with "thanks."

The concert at the Conservatoire went very well and I was pleased with the response and the congeniality of the other guitarists and musicians in the audience. It was a great experience even though the audience was limited to a couple hundred people due to the size of the concert hall, but it was still a rousing success, I thought. I hung around for a while and discussed the state of the classical guitar in the world. Most of the students spoke English surprisingly well, unlike in the United States where many don't speak other languages. This was Europe and because the countries are in such close proximity to each other everyone has to speak multiple languages.

Next was Paris where I had a few friends in the city. I very much looked forward to enjoying the city. I would have three performances there set up by our French contact, Arnaud Duchamp, a close friend and wonderful guitarist and lutenist and quite a character and operator. Arnaud has his fingers into a lot of things, some of which I don't ask about. But he is wonderful company. On to the city of lights!

CHAPTER 5

Paris

Paris was and is a very special city to me. It was where Eve and I spent our honeymoon visiting the Louvre, Eiffel Tower, Arc de Triomphe and of course some of the finest restaurants in the world. I had hoped to return sooner to the city of lights, but it was not possible, so I was thrilled to be back so many years later, but without Eve it was bittersweet.

After riding the Eurostar, I checked in at the Hotel de Paris in the center of Paris. Arnaud Duchamp was ready to meet me. I had brought him over from Paris to perform at the University in New York two years ago and helped promote his Weil Recital Hall debut at Carnegie Hall. He was excited to see me and help in any way he could to facilitate my time in Paris. We met for dinner and discussed the upcoming concerts on September 27th, 28th, and 30th. He told me the first two were just a warmup for the big one at the Olympia concert hall, the oldest music hall in Paris. Arnaud said he invited the entire conservatory class to the Olympia as a free concert to be paid for by the university, so he was sure we would have a nice size crowd since that was over five hundred tickets sold to students already. I was psyched for the concerts!

When we spoke, Arnaud mentioned "I've been contacted by a representative of a business consortium who said they want to meet you to discuss some further possibilities in Europe. They also want to know more about you personally for some reason, that seemed strange to me." I asked what those possibilities were, and he said, "I have no idea what they could be, I guess we will find out when we meet up." I said, "I have no problem getting together with them as long as it fits comfortably into my schedule." I asked if he knew their name since I wanted to know more about them. He said, "They're known as the World Trade Company or WTC, and he will speak to them and let me know." I figured there was no harm in listening to what they had to say and finding out more about them. Little did I know who they really were.

The first two concerts were at the Paris Conservatory and the Guitar Society of France. Both went well and I was glad I had some time to work out some of the kinks in my hands from traveling so it was fun to perform these. The Olympia concert was different and a big one for me since reviewers would be there and I wanted to use it as a nice springboard for my concerts in Rome and Madrid. Arnaud said we would have dinner with a couple of representatives from the consortium on October 1st after the Olympia concert and I told him that was fine with me. I asked him if he knew their names but Arnaud just said, "They were known as the World Trade Company and that's all I know." It was all a mystery to both of us.

My performance at the Olympia went fabulously and I felt great about it afterwards. The audience was very warm and receptive and even gave me a standing ovation at the end. I added a few encores, one of which included *Gymnopedie* by Erik Satie, a crowd favorite of French audiences. My Spanish guitar, Pedro de Miguel, sounded bright and lively for the Spanish repertoire while my German guitar, Armin Hanika, also sounded great with a deep resonant tone in the hall for the Bach *Chaconne*. I was pleased and relieved it went so well. Tomorrow I would meet with the consortium and see what this was all about. For now, I was content with the way things were going and wanted to keep it that way. Little did I know my equilibrium would be thrown off very soon by the upcoming meeting with the mysterious WTC.

CHAPTER 6

The Package

Upon waking up the next morning at the hotel I went online and read the reviews of my debut at the Olympia. They were all positive to varying degrees depending on the reviewer so I was pleased there were really no negative reviews and one great one that I could use for future promotion. Jeanine was collecting reviews and forwarding them to the public relations people in Rome and Madrid so they could use them to attract audiences and sell tickets. As far as I knew she was back in the states after our last encounter but was still responding to my emails. Hopefully that episode was closed, and we could continue to work together but who knows, women are very unpredictable—especially when they have set their sights on their target.

As I was getting dressed, I took a moment to look in the mirror and judge my appearance. I wanted to see what the audience saw when I walked out onstage. My wavy black hair had grown a bit and had hints of grey but not much, not so bad for a guy in his forties. My face looked a bit tired, and it showed around my eyes, but since I have a dark complexion, it seemed to not show as much. I had put on a few pounds on my five-foot, eleven inch, one-hundred-and-ninety-pound frame before I left for the tour, but those seemed to have come off. Touring tends to make one lose weight due to the constant movement, stress, and missed meals. I was in pretty good shape for the most part at this point. I was looking forward to getting back to my rigorous exercise routine when I returned to New York, it helps to be in tour shape. My goal was to use this tour as a steppingstone to further performances so it was imperative that I stay in shape for what may lie ahead.

Before having dinner with the representatives from the consortium Arnaud invited me out for a drink. We were to meet at a small bar just off the Champs-Élysées at 5pm to debrief how the Paris concerts went. During the day I just packed and rested and did some shopping. I wanted to buy Eve something nice in Paris, so it took some doing to find the right item. I knew she was looking for a new handbag so I bought her a small designer bag made by Jean Patou that could only be bought in France. I was sure she knew the designer since she had mentioned it to me. Maybe that was a subliminal hint she sent me? Well apparently, it got through.

5pm rolled around and there was Arnaud outside the bar waiting for me. We sat down at the bar, and I ordered one of my whiskey usuals, a Manhattan, and started to discuss the tour and how well it went. I asked him if he knew anything further about these people we were meeting tonight and he said, "No, they just contacted me out of the blue with no other information." I told him "It seems very strange, what do they want with me?" For now, I would just go with it. We were meeting them at 7pm down the block at a nice restaurant even by Paris standards.

We arrived early and were seated by the Maître D at a private table in an alcove of the restaurant. The restaurant was the world-renowned Chez Napoléon, a five-star Michelin restaurant in the heart of Paris so this was a different vibe than your usual place in Paris. When Sergei and Luca walked into the restaurant, I knew this was going to be no ordinary dinner meeting. They were from the World Trade Company that represented other companies as part of a consortium. Arnaud and I stood up and greeted them with handshakes around and we proceeded to be seated. Apparently, this private area the WTC used for quiet meetings with clients and who knows who else.

Sergei introduced himself as the vice-president of the company and went on to explain that the World Trade Company did business in fifty-two countries around the world. Its main function was to be the facilitator of various types of goods from one country to another. The goods could be anything from food and absolute necessities to fine antiques and collectibles. It all depended on what the buyer needed or wanted. He said, "The WTC makes it happen for the right price." He also said, "We believe in the arts as well and donate regularly through our philanthropic department." This all sounded legit so far. I wondered how far the services went though for the right price?

Luca was in charge of security for the company, and he looked the part. You wouldn't want to meet him in a dark alley; he was a mountain of a man and somewhat intimidating. Large hands, muscular body and at least six foot five or so. Someone I would see regularly unfortunately it seemed. Sergei on the other hand was small and balding, very squatty, about five foot six or so, and was quite a contrast to Luca, making them kind of an odd couple.

Sergei asked, "Mr. Lanbourne, how is the tour going being we are one of your sponsors?" "Very well," I responded. Sergei then asked a few other personal questions about my marriage and past life that were unrelated to the tour while we had drinks and appetizers that he ordered with the snap of his fingers. His line of questioning seemed odd. After we had ordered our main courses, he said he had some business he would like to discuss with me. I said, "I'm all ears." Sergei went on to say "We are looking for someone who would not attract attention to deliver a package to the United States Embassy in Madrid. We chose you since no one would suspect a concert guitarist to deliver the package." To go along with the delivery, there would be ample compensation, and he assured me that nothing was illegal, it just had to do with the WTC being able to outmaneuver a competitor and that the competition always had eyes on their employees. That's why they wanted someone outside the company to deliver the package."

I didn't know what to say at that point except to ask "How did you happen to choose me? I am not the only musician in Europe." Sergei said Juan Carlos Garcia recommended me as a likely candidate to do it and since I lived in the United States there would be no possibility of a conflict with the WTC's competitors. I asked if I would be able to think about it and get back to him, he said he needed to know by ten o'clock tomorrow morning. I said that was fine and our food was served at that point. After having coffee, Sergei picked up the check and we were about to leave when Luca said menacingly, "Mr. Lanbourne, I would think very seriously about accepting this assignment. It would be very serious if you didn't and might affect your ability to finish the tour successfully." Those were the only words he had said all night, and they were meant to send a message to me. Obviously, this was part of their plan. It put me on high alert as to what was going on here. I just needed to figure out how to get out of this without offending anyone.

Arnaud, a typical Frenchman, beret, angular nose and all, went for an after-dinner drink with me to talk about what had just happened. He said "I was taken off guard by the whole thing since it had nothing to do with the actual tour or, for that matter, the arts. I'm not sure what they are up to but Jonathan if you need any further help in the future regarding this, feel free to reach out to me. I know people who can help if the situation calls for it." I told him what Luca had said to me in private when we were leaving. Arnaud said "Mon Dieu, I am now very concerned about this, please keep me informed." I said "I'm not sure what the consequences will be if I turn them down. I am scared it will turn out badly for me if I do." Arnaud suggested calling Juan Carlos and speaking with him about it. I said I would reach out when I got back to the hotel. I wasn't leaving Paris until the day after, October 3rd, so I had some time to kill. We said our goodbyes and I said I would let him know how it went. Arnaud felt somewhat responsible for putting together the dinner, but I knew it would have happened with or without him and he was just stuck in the middle of it.

When I returned to the hotel, I called Juan Carlos. He picked up after three rings and said he was expecting me to call. I asked, "who is the WTC? They seem like thugs. I have real concerns as to what is behind all they are asking me to do. Luca threatened me as well." Juan Carlos replied, "as far as I know they are a reputable company, and I've dealt with them before without any problems occurring. It's up to you, I just thought it would be a good way for you to earn some extra money while you are here." I replied, "it just seems shady to me and doesn't make sense." I thanked him and said I wasn't sure at this point. When I got off the phone with him, I called Eve in New York. It was late but she picked up so she didn't have a lot of time to speak. I told her "The main sponsor of the tour wants me to deliver a package to the United States Embassy without an explanation as to what it is. They say they need someone outside of their organization since they are followed by their competitors. There would be ample compensation for doing it but it seems off to me." She immediately said "Jonathan this sounds fishy, do you really want to do this? There could be risk involved that you are not taking into consideration." I told her I pretty much felt the same and would reject the offer the next morning. Women's intuition is almost always correct.

Sergei called me at exactly 10am the next morning and I answered. He asked "Mr. Lanbourne, have you made your decision? I need to know now so we can plan." I told him "I'm sorry but I am not comfortable delivering a package that I have no idea what the contents are and will pass on the offer." As I thanked him for the offer he said "You should reconsider the offer, it is something you need to give deep thought to. There are ramifications for you if you refuse us." I told him,"my decision is final and I don't appreciate the tone of your response." I then thanked him again, trying to be diplomatic. A few minutes after I got off the phone with Sergei there was a knock on my door. What was about to happen would be right out of a gangster movie. One that I was a part of, unwillingly.

CHAPTER 7

Rome

I went to the door and looked through the peep hole—it was Luca. He said "Mr. Lanbourne, please open the door, I need to speak with you." I answered that I did not feel comfortable opening the door to him. He said if I didn't, he would have to take drastic measures and knock it down if necessary. I had no other choice but to let him in. I didn't want to test him. I remember Luca's exact words to this day; "Mr. Lanbourne, you will accept our offer and there will be a package delivered to your hotel in Madrid that you **will** deliver to the embassy. If you insist on not doing what we ask of you there will be consequences. Let's just say, and pardon my English, we know people who can cause great harm to you and your family members. Let's just leave it at that. We will, of course, honor our end of the bargain to compensate you well. We had hoped you would have accepted when we asked, and it didn't come to this, but as head of security at WTC, I will enforce what needs to be done to protect the company. We are not asking any longer." I was aghast at what was said and basically shaking in my boots. Nothing else was said in that regard and I knew I had to just do what they asked, at least for now. Luca said they would be in touch with instructions and that I should tell no one, then he left and thankfully left the door to my room intact.

The next day came and I caught a flight from Charles De Gaulle airport to Leonardo da Vinci airport in Rome. The flight took around three hours, so I had time to think about what had happened. Why me? What did I have to do with any of this? I arrived at the Colosseum Hotel in the heart of Rome and considered my plight. I still had to perform two concerts in Rome before Madrid, so I had to concentrate to do my best. For the rest I would have to hope for the best outcome.

My contact in Rome was Sophia Caruso, an Italian concert promoter who knew the landscape well. She was a very attractive, middle-aged Italian woman with dark hair and olive complexion, and a very shapely figure like a Madonna. I would be performing at the Conservatory of Rome first and then the more important one at Auditorium Parco della Musica, a contemporary complex for cultural events. The recitals would take place Friday, October 5th at the Conservatory and Sunday, October 7th at the Auditorium. Promotion had already been done for them from my previous reviews so I was sure there would be a nice audience there. Sophia told me everything looked good for the concerts. She also told me Jeanine had contacted her and said she would be coming to the main event concert on Sunday. That concerned me. Why was she coming here? Here we go again. I tried not to think about that since I had a more pressing situation to try and figure out. I had to come up with an alternate plan.

The next day I had dinner with Sophia at a wonderful Italian restaurant in Rome. Their specialty was the cuisine that Rome was known for. They specialized in Carbonara, a dish that features a creamy sauce that's made with pancetta, garlic, pasta water, cheese, and eggs. That, with a fabulous bottle of 2008 Brunello de Montalcino red wine made the dinner, of course, off the charts. Getting back to reality, alarmingly, Sophia said "The WTC has been in touch with me saying they have invested in the tour and wanted to know if everything was going okay in Rome." She then asked me if it was true that they had invested. I had no choice but to say it was. I then asked, "Sophia, do you know anything about the WTC and whether they are legit or not?" She answered, "I really don't know them, I have heard their name through a colleague but know nothing, I will answer them and let them know everything is going well as planned." Sophia asked, "How do you feel about the upcoming concerts, are you confident about them going well?" I just said, "I always feel confident but once you are onstage anything can happen." She offered help to me whenever I needed it, and I thanked her for that and said I would be in touch.

The concert at the Conservatory of Rome did not go as well as I had hoped. I was distracted and didn't perform up to my standards. I knew I had to bear down regardless of what was going on for my performance at the Auditorium Parco della Musica, so I went back to the hotel to practice my program and concentrate. I had to isolate the hard parts of the program and practice them separately. The next day would be here soon enough and there would be plenty of other things to deal with. A plan started to be formulated in my head as to how I would proceed with the WTC's demand; I just had to figure out a way to execute it. I decided to explore it and assess the risk involved. What was the chance I could pull it off? Only time would tell.

I phoned Eve but she didn't pick up so I headed down to the bar where I could do my best thinking. Who knew what tomorrow would bring, but I had to be as prepared as possible for it. This time I ordered a Vodka Martini, shaken, not stirred. I was beginning to feel like a secret agent. How crazy was that? What was I turning into? James Bond?

CHAPTER 8

Rome Continued

I woke up early the next day to warm up my hands. I didn't sleep well at all; I spent the whole night tossing and turning. Sophia was going to come by at five o'clock so we would arrive at the Auditorium early to try out the hall. Once there I sat in the hall with my guitar foot stool set so when I walked out on stage it would be the correct height without me having to make any last-minute adjustments. I was determined to perform well tonight regardless of the circumstances. I thought, "screw them", I was not going to let Sergei and Luca get into my head. First, I had to perform well, then plan my plan. It wouldn't be easy, but I needed backups so that I would get out of this in one piece. The chances were diminishing by the hour.

Jeanine showed up at the hall and came to my dressing room. She gave me a peck on the cheek, and I asked her why she flew out again, thinking it was a leading question. She said in Brussels she and Juan Carlos had gone out to dinner and hit it off well, so he invited her to the Rome concert. I didn't recall Juan Carlos being in Brussels. Anyway, how could she turn down a fully paid trip to Rome? So here she was. She asked how I was, and I told her I was hanging in there. I guess her crush on me is no longer, or is this just a way to get to me? In any case I thanked her for coming to give me support. She also let me know Juan Carlos told her the World Trade Company had bought hundreds of tickets for the concert to fill the hall. I didn't know what to say at that point, so I just said, "that's great." I guess the WTC wanted to keep tabs on me to make sure I showed up in Madrid to deliver their package. She wished me "break a leg" and I proceeded to do just that.

I walked out onstage to a full house and knew the pressure was on me to give a technical and interpretive top-notch performance. I was determined again not to let the circumstances affect my performance. Hey, this was my life, my career that I had worked so hard to establish. I couldn't let anything get in my way, even the WTC, whatever they were. I positioned my hands and off I went.

The Sanz suite went by like a blur. Being a collection of Spanish Baroque dances, it flowed from one to the next. I felt good and forgot all about what was going on. Next came the Bach Chaconne. I knew that the less I thought about it, the better I would perform. It flowed like never before due to me not overthinking it. Maybe what was going on would help me perform even better since my focus was on that and not on performing? Was I learning something here? Once again, I just went out and had fun with the second half of the concert since they were lighter pieces, although the Albeniz pieces did present some challenges. I finished it off with my *Rumba Improv in the style of the Gypsy Kings* as an encore. It went over great; the audience gave me a standing ovation.

After the concert, Sophia, Jeanine, and Juan Carlos came backstage to congratulate me. I knew I had performed well, maybe better than ever. They suggested we go out for drinks and desserts. I knew this would be a good opportunity to quiz Juan Carlos about the WTC. I wasn't sure if he was in on it or just an innocent bystander being used by them. I said I wanted to drop my guitars back at the hotel and change so we would meet there and let Sophia take us to a place she knows well. Having a native Roman with you helps. When in Rome do as the Romans do, as the saying goes.

We went to a bar called Annie Hall. It was named that due to the owner's infatuation with the movie from the 1970's. The ambience and drinks were a relief from the day. I asked Juan Carlos "How did you and Jeanine meet since I didn't recall you being in Brussels." He said, "I was in touch with her about the arrangement for the concert but couldn't attend the performance due to a previous obligation." I then went on to drill him about how he knew the WTC and why they bought so many tickets. Juan Carlos responded, "They are a large funder of the European Union Cultural Council and I was very appreciative to have their support." I then pushed the issue and asked him "what is your involvement with the WTC since it seems you are more involved than just with the Council." He responded, "I have no other involvement with them other than the Council and don't really know the people running it." I thought his answer was strange but left it at that and didn't bring up our conversation about the package delivery and neither did he. I had two full days left in Rome before leaving for Madrid on Wednesday, October 10th, so I wanted to do some digging to see what I could find out about the WTC and Juan Carlos. As we parted for the evening, he pulled me aside and reminded me not to say anything about the package delivery just to be safe. I told him I was well aware of that and that he needn't be concerned. I thought to myself "what the hell is his involvement with all this that he wants me to be silent?"

The next day I woke up, had a great hotel breakfast, and was determined to find out what I could about the WTC. Off I went and asked Sophia if we could have coffee that day and she agreed. I wanted to find a resource that could tell me more about the WTC. My cover for Sophia would be that I was interested in meeting them and thanking them for the support of my tour, but first I asked her if she knew anyone who knew of them so I could be prepared. She said she thought so and would reach out to him to see if he was available to speak with me. He was a reporter and did some digging on the WTC a few years ago. His name was Jordan Long, and he worked for an international publication here in Rome. Sophia said to give her a couple of hours and she would get back to me. She also told me Jordan was a little spooked by his WTC digging and sometimes hesitant to speak with people about it. I thanked her and she said she would be in touch. Maybe this was the connection I was looking for to give me the scoop on the WTC. Maybe there was more there than meets the eye?

CHAPTER 9

The Meeting

I went back to the hotel to await Sophia's call and sure enough about an hour later my phone rang. She said Jordan had agreed to meet with me but at a secure place of his choosing and that I had to come alone. He would send the location later in the afternoon before he left his flat around 5pm. Sophia said she gave him my phone number so he could contact me directly. I thanked her for that and for all her help while I was here in Rome. She told me to be careful; Jordan was on to something that got squashed from the powers above at the newspaper so maybe some things are left best alone.

At around 4:45pm I received a text from Jordan telling me to meet him at 5pm behind the Colosseum at a bench near the old ruins. He would be wearing a grey blazer and had brown hair and glasses. If I wasn't there by 5:05pm he said he would leave. I quickly got myself together and since I was staying at the Colosseum Hotel, I was right around the corner from where he wanted to meet. He also asked me to look around and make sure I wasn't being followed. Being that I don't work in espionage, this was not exactly up my alley, but I would try and make sure there weren't any suspicious characters watching me.

I arrived at the bench at 4:55pm and saw a man approaching that fit Jordan's description. Sure enough, it was him and he motioned for me to sit down. He was as he described himself but also tall and lanky and looked like a nerdy journalist with a baseball cap on. He went on to ask "what is your relationship with the World Trade Company, how are you involved?" I told him "they are a supporter of my concert tour through the European Union Cultural Council, but they asked me and are actually forcing me to do something for them that I was not comfortable doing." I told Jordan "I can't be specific at this point since I was told to keep silent or else something might happen to me, hence the desire to find out more about them and what I was involved with."

Jordan said "I will take you into my confidence, but you have to swear you won't involve me in any way." He said, "two years ago I was researching the WTC for an article for the European Times. Being a free-lance journalist, I was able to choose my subjects and submit them. What I came up with was very disturbing. The WTC is not a real trade company at all, they are involved with money laundering schemes, espionage, terrorism, and all kinds of illegal activities. They are basically mercenaries for foreign governments looking to let's just say, do bad things. They operate under a cloak of secrecy and use everyday people as couriers to do their bad deeds, unwittingly. It sounds like you are one of those

40

selected." Our conversation seemed very tense. Jordan was nervous and looking to leave as soon as possible. He was just doing Sophia a favor he said.

Jordan continued to say "when I submitted my article to the Times it was squashed by the executives above saying that I didn't have enough proof. I had a mountain of emails and sworn testimonies from sources that corroborated my work, yet the article was rejected." After hearing from the Times, he went home to also find his two dogs were killed by an unknown assailant. They broke into his apartment but didn't take anything, just murdered his dogs to send a message. After calling the Polizia, they said they had no leads as to who did this. For all he knew, they might have been involved as well. In thinking about it, he said "I should have gone higher up to Interpol immediately. The local police are notorious for being bought off by criminal groups."

Since then, Jordan said he has laid low and didn't go any further with the article, fearing for his life. At that point I felt a feeling of dread come over me. Jordan told me "whatever they ask you to do, just do it and get the hell out after that if possible. These aren't people to be reasoned with." I told Jordan "Yes, I found that out in my encounter with them. They threatened me and my family, and I seem to have no choice unless I take it to Interpol." Jordan replied, "That is a risk that if they find out could be worse for you than just doing what they ask." I thanked him for the information and meeting with me and asked, "Is there any way I can reach out to you with any further questions if necessary?" He said nervously that he appreciated my situation and apologized but didn't want to be involved any further. He said he had received threatening texts as well to back off or else. I didn't know at the time, but this was the last I would see or hear from Jordan.

I went back to the hotel even further discouraged, but thinking I needed to get through this. The following morning, I was flying out from Leonardo da Vinci airport to Adolfo Suárez Madrid-Barajas Airport in Madrid, about a three-hour flight, so I needed to get packed and get out early. I had to do some research and planning before I arrived in Madrid. Who knew what would present itself to me there? On the plane I signed on to the wi-fi and did some digging. What I would find out wasn't good and didn't bode well for me.

CHAPTER 10

Madrid

On the plane to Madrid, I weighed my options. Do I just do as I am told, or do I open the package and contact the authorities? There was no easy answer here, but I knew what I had to do. In Madrid my contact was no other than Juan Carlos Garcia so I thought maybe I could extract some more information from him to help me make my decision. In the meantime, I needed to prepare for the concert in Madrid at the National Music Auditorium on October 13th and my concert at the castle in Segovia on October 17th. I expected to hear from the WTC upon my arrival in Madrid as well about the package. I was sure they would be all over me.

Upon my arrival at the Hotel España in Madrid I asked the concierge if there were any messages for me. He said there were not, so I went to my room, unpacked and sat down to practice for an hour. I needed the comfort of my guitars to provide me with mental stability for the time ahead. Things were quiet at the moment, and it felt nice to have some temporary sanity. I was waiting for the other shoe to drop with the package being delivered and whatever was going to go into that. While researching on the plane, I learned that the WTC operates in fifty-two countries across the world. Their reach was far greater than I ever imagined, which meant there was no hiding from them.

At 5pm or so my phone rang. It was Sophia with some potentially bad news. Jordan Long didn't show up for a meeting with her yesterday and had gone missing. She said, "his phone goes directly to voicemail and the police said it's too early to look for him since it must be twenty-four hours or longer, but this is not like Jordan to miss a meeting. He is obsessively reliable in that way." I thanked her for letting me know and she said she would let me know of any updates. I feared for the worst since he probably had a target on his back and took a risk meeting with me. If they saw me with Jordan that day at the bench, I would have a target as well on my back. I would have to adjust my plan to mitigate my risk somehow. I just wasn't completely sure how?

I grabbed dinner at the hotel. Juan Carlos had invited me out to dinner the next day to talk about things, so I was free tonight. I practiced my program, especially the Rodrigo that I would perform at the castle, and hoped for the best in hearing from Sophia. No package had been delivered yet, so my anxiety level was growing. I hit the bar before bed to grab a Macallan 12 to ease my anxiety and went upstairs. Things were just too eerily uneventful. Maybe that was good, but I wanted events to move along so at some point I could get past this situation. I was riddled with anxiety.

The next morning Sophia called with bad news. Jordan's body had been found outside of Rome by a riverbed. He had been shot twice in the head. She was called down to identify the body since her phone number and calls were the last ones on his cell phone. I, of course, flipped out hearing this. I felt sick to my stomach and remembered what Jordan had said, it was a warning to me! Apparently, the WTC was some sort of mob organization, but I wasn't sure who they were working for or with. What government hired them and why? Sophia was crying on the phone and said, "even though I didn't know Jordan that well, it's still very upsetting, I feel somewhat responsible for his death since I set him up with you." I replied, "Sophia, there is no way you could have known it would turn out this way, it's not your fault, don't be hard on yourself." I thanked her for letting me know and told her to let me know if they found out anything further. My life depended on it as well. She went on to say the police were investigating it and if I knew Italy, they would not find anything if it was somehow mob related. She was sure the WTC had paid them off.

Almost immediately after hanging up with Sophia the phone rang again. This time it was the front desk telling me a package had arrived, and they asked whether I wanted it delivered to my room. I told them I would come get it, since I wanted to scan the lobby and see if anything looked fishy down there. I left my room and went down to the front desk to retrieve the package. If anyone was watching me, I couldn't tell so I just took it up to my room. The package was about twelve by twelve inches and there was an envelope attached to the outside that said "Mr. Jonathan Lanbourne, please open and read."

The letter read as follows, "please deliver this package to the United State Embassy, attention Robert Somerfield, assistant to the ambassador, on October 14th and do not, under any circumstances, open the package. You will have top priority clearance upon showing your passport, to enter the building and deliver the package directly to him. After delivering, please depart immediately."

I had a decision to make. Was I going to open the package and see what I was delivering or just do as they instructed me? Both ways were risky, but my plan was in place already. Maybe if I knew what it was, I would be able to make a decision and report it to the correct authorities. The problem though was, who was that? The United States Embassy might be compromised, and the Italian police might be in bed with the WTC as well, depending on who I spoke with. And on the other hand, if I delivered the package, would I be an accomplice to a crime of international espionage of huge proportions with massive implications? I decided I would make my decision tonight after having dinner with Juan Carlos. Maybe I could get a read on him that would shed some light on it one way or another. I would wait for that to make my decision. At this point, what did I have to lose? Time wasn't on my side though, so I had to move with a sense of urgency.

CHAPTER 11

The Decision

Juan Carlos and I met at Plaza España, a wonderful, well-known restaurant in the heart of Madrid. He had booked a private room where we could speak without interference. I love Spanish cuisine and the various dishes we had: shrimp in a garlic sauce, paella dishes of all kinds on rice, and of course, the drink of Spain, sangria. Unfortunately for me, I couldn't really enjoy it very much due to the circumstances that consumed me. Hopefully another time I would be free to partake again once all this had passed. I was beginning to wonder if that was even possible.

When we sat down at the dinner table, we ordered drinks and appetizers and then Juan Carlos asked me all the formalities, how the tour was going and so on. I told him I thought it was going as well as could be expected. He said he wasn't sure how to take that since he had heard and seen only good things out of me on stage. I was, of course, alluding to the other unexpected ask of me on the tour outside of

47

my artistic activities. I planned to bring up that subject after dinner when the time was right.

We had cocktails and tapas appetizers and then our main meal was served. I ordered Paella with seafood, and we enjoyed a bottle of Marques de Caceres Sauvignon Blanc wine. As the time for dessert and coffee came, I had to figure out how I was going to broach the subject of the delivery. It appeared I didn't have to. Juan Carlos asked, "So did you receive the package that you have to deliver yet?" I told him I did and was conflicted as to why I was being forced to deliver it. He asked why I used the word "forced." I said I was told not to speak about it to anyone. Juan Carlos seemed puzzled, which led me to believe he wasn't in on it with the WTC. Then again, he could just be acting. I asked, "what do you know about this package and why did you recommend me to deliver it?" He just answered, "truly, Jonathan, I know nothing at all about this package and the people involved, just that you were a likely candidate to deliver it for them. It all seemed very innocent and straightforward." If he knew anything he was not going to tell me for sure.

We finished our coffee and dessert, and as we were departing, Juan Carlos said he would check into what I had alluded to about being forced to deliver the package to see if he could find out anything further. He wished me luck for tomorrow's concert and said he would speak to me after it was over so I could concentrate on my performance. I went back to the hotel and hit the bar for my usual Macallan 12, so I would be able to take my mind off the package and sleep. I would get up the next day, concentrate on my program for the concert, and deal with whatever afterwards. Even though I would be focusing on the concert in Madrid, I had already made up my mind in my head what I was going to do. It seemed I had no choice if I was to protect myself against any retaliation from the WTC.

The next day came, I warmed up my hands and brain and tried to relax for most of the day. I went to the National Music Auditorium around 6pm to give myself enough time to mentally prepare for the concert. Once again, Jeanine showed up in my dressing room unannounced, having been invited to Spain by Juan Carlos of course. I wasn't surprised this time, but I had more important matters on my mind. She once again gave me a peck on the cheek and wished me luck and I thanked her again. 8pm rolled around and I went out onstage, somewhat numb and mindless, and just dove in.

CHAPTER 12

The Decision, Part Two

As before, it seemed the music played itself. I was a spectator watching my hands perform all the moves flawlessly. I was actually getting to a deeper level of performance than I ever had before. It was almost subconscious. Again, I discovered, the less I thought about it, the better it went. It was almost mystical to me, something definitely to be explored further. The audience, which was smaller than expected, was very receptive and I received a standing ovation. I was on a high from the applause and audience enthusiasm. After two encores I was finished and headed for the dressing room. The next day I was due to deliver the package to the embassy, so I had to do some thinking and planning. I had to get past this performance, as good as it was.

When I returned to the hotel, I went up to the room to leave my guitars and then returned back downstairs to the bar for you know what, Macallan 12. To my surprise there was Juan Carlos and Jeanine at a high-top table. They saw me walk in and immediately invited me over to join them. I was a bit reluctant but thought maybe I could pick up some other hints from Juan Carlos as to his involvement with the WTC. It was worth a shot.

As I sipped my whiskey, Juan Carlos congratulated me on a great concert. He was sure the reviews would be great. Jeanine also joined in congratulating me, she of course, looked extremely hot. The usual, tight blouse, short skirt, boots, showing off her cleavage and legs. Juan Carlos then went on to say that he called Sergei about the package delivery and asked if I was coerced into doing it. Sergei denied it vehemently and said I agreed of my own free will to do it. I was wondering here at the table if I had done the wrong thing mentioning anything to Juan Carlos since I was supposed to keep my mouth shut. I hoped I wasn't going to receive a visit from Luca about it. Juan Carlos said he had received a message regarding the concert at the castle in Segovia. They had requested only one piece of music: the *Invocation and Dance* by Joaquin Rodrigo, apparently a favorite of the sponsor of the concert. I thought how odd, the whole concert would take fifteen minutes or so. I quickly downed my drink and ordered another, this time a double. I was going to need it apparently.

After leaving Juan Carlos and Jeanine to go back to my room I scoped out the lobby to see if anyone looked suspicious. Once again, not being trained in espionage, no one looked strange. When I returned to my room, I looked at the package. I had made my decision and would open it carefully so I could reseal it just as it looked when it arrived. The questions were, what would I do if I found something that had to be reported? And who would I report it to? I felt I needed to know what I was involved in here. Otherwise, I would not be able to figure out an escape plan to cover my butt. This was the only way out I felt.

I brought the package over to a table that was in the room and looked at the wrapping carefully. It was in a small shopping bag, most likely to disguise its contents, and had an outer layer that could be unzipped. I took it out of the bag and unzipped the outer layer. Inside was a metal container that looked like a safety deposit box. I looked it over and saw that a combination was needed to open it. I held it up to my ear and was able to hear a slight humming inside. There was definitely some kind of device in there. As for what kind, I couldn't even venture to guess. Then I had a thought, what if I was able to see it through a CT scanner like they use at the airport? How would I find one? Thinking back, Arnaud had told me he had a cousin who worked at the airport here in Madrid in the baggage area. I would call Arnaud and see if I could get this done prior to delivering it tomorrow. It all depended on what Arnaud's cousin could do for me. This would enable me to determine the level of threat in this.

I immediately called Arnaud and explained I had a package I wanted scanned to see if I would have a problem getting through security at the airport. I wanted to see if I could get it scanned in advance to make sure. Arnaud thought about it asking if this was the one from the WTC in our meeting. I had no choice but to tell him the truth and said yes it was. He said he would call his cousin, Jean Pierre, to see if he would be able to help me. Arnaud said he would call me back; I told him it was time sensitive so ASAP would be great and to please use discretion with Jean Pierre, only on a need-to-know basis.

Approximately ten minutes after speaking with Arnaud I received a phone call from Jean Pierre. He asked me some questions and said since I was a close friend of Arnaud's he would do me the favor, but it had to be kept quiet. He then asked, "can you get to the airport early tomorrow morning? I will have access to the scanners at 8am." I said of course. What I had to figure out was how I would explain this to Jean Pierre once we looked at the scan. That was the tricky part. I could come clean and tell the truth or figure out a way to get around the truth that he would accept. I knew I had to do this one way or another to make sure I wasn't doing something that had international implications. This was all part of my plan. I would see where it went and stick with it.

The next morning, I rushed to the 8am meeting with Jean Pierre. He said he would meet me in Baggage Area Six and was wearing a work reflector outfit as is worn in the outside baggage areas. I found Jean Pierre easy enough; he was a short stocky Frenchman. I asked him "How did you end up here in Madrid?" He responded in his thick French accent "I fell in love with a woman from Madrid, how else? Love makes a man do crazy things." We went directly to an area that had scanners outside of the security area and he told me to place the package on a platform so he could scan it.

I watched with Jean Pierre as the scanner moved over the package and stopped in the middle. Jean Pierre looked at the scan and looked at me and asked, "what is this device?" I then had to make the decision to come clean or talk my way out of it. I decided the former. I told him I was given an ultimatum to deliver this to the United State Embassy today and didn't know what was in the package. He said he might have to call in the higher ups to address this. At that point, I made the decision to go with it. It was the best and only choice I had to make. Jean Pierre looked very concerned while he made the necessary call.

Jean Pierre had contacted the head of airport security, Alejandro Vargas, to meet with us. Alejandro was tall and handsome and looked like the type that did things by the books. He then led me into a private room where I was with Jean Pierre and the package. Alejandro then went on to ask, "we need a full explanation, Mr. Lanbourne, of how this package got into your possession and what you are being asked to do. This is very important since it seems something illegal is going on here." Feeling pressured, I spilled the beans and told him pretty much how it went down with the WTC and that I was unsure of what to do. That was why I am here. At this point, I was getting fed up with the whole ordeal and just wanted it to end.

Alejandro said he would need to contact Interpol since it involved multiple countries in Europe. He told us to wait in the holding room until he heard from them. Within the hour Interpol had sent an agent over to speak with us and look at the package again under the scanner. Mario Sincenzi was a technical expert on espionage devices and disarming them in the field. An Italian by birth, he had lived in six different countries in the last ten years. This made him ideal for this type of work, being familiar with all the European countries and their languages. After looking at the device under the scanner he said he surmised that it might be a device that omits electronic waves like the ones that were deployed during the Havana Syndrome in Cuba some twenty years ago. When activated, the device had the capability of making anyone who comes in contact with the waves very ill and possibly cause death. Mario said he would have to contact his supervisor to see how they wanted to proceed. At that point, I was in a no-win situation. I had to go with it and hope for the best. If I got Interpol involved maybe I could get out of this cleanly. The odds were against me though. The next day or so would tell my fate.

CHAPTER 13

The Plan

Mario returned with more information and a plan. Interpol, with the help of the CIA, had surmised that the delivery of the package had something to do with the visit of Senator Tommy Lee from Alabama on October 18th. Senator Lee was on the Armed Services Committee, so Interpol did not want to take a chance of the device being activated on that day. In order to acquire more information to confirm the exact individuals who were behind this, they wanted me to deliver the package as scheduled. It was October 14th, so they had four days to investigate further and if necessary, evacuate the embassy before the 18th. I agreed to the plan and would deliver it to Robert Somerfield as instructed. Mario also said Interpol would assign two agents to follow me just in case. They couldn't stay too close since the WTC would get suspicious if they figured out who they were but would take whatever precautions necessary. Interpol also provided me with a burner cell phone so they could trace and contact me if needed. I was to always leave it on.

I showed up at the embassy that was situated among other government buildings in Madrid around 1pm in the afternoon, trying to make sure I wasn't followed. The guard in the booth outside as I passed through the gates took my name and ran my passport to confirm my identity. He then pointed me to a walkway that apparently went to the back of the building. I was a bit surprised since the metal detectors were within my view as I entered the front of the building. Was I being set up for something? It seemed odd but I followed the guard's instructions.

When I got to the end of the walkway a door opened, and a man came out and introduced himself as Robert Somerfield. He looked like a typical seasoned diplomat: tall with dress shirt and pants, no tie, and patches of grey in his hair. Without inviting me in, he took the bag with the package from me and said, "please leave now and don't look back, act as just a messenger and this never took place." I did as I was told and high tailed it out of there as fast as possible. The whole delivery was very suspect and suspicious.

When I returned to the hotel, I hit the bar to calm down- it was Macallan 12 time. I knew I needed to practice the Rodrigo also before the castle concert on October 17th since I hadn't touched it in a few days, but I knew I was in no mental state to do so. I would get up in the morning and tackle it; I had a couple of days. A few hours later when I got back to my room the phone rang, it was Jeanine. She asked if I wanted to meet her and Juan Carlos at a tapas bar near the hotel in an hour. Since I needed some company, I said yes and then proceeded to call Eve. It was late for her in New York since she gets up every morning at five in the morning, so she didn't answer. I just left her a message that everything was going well, and I looked forward to getting back home. I didn't want her to worry about what was going on here in Madrid. I was sure she would be mad at me for not telling her the whole story in advance, but I didn't see the point to do it now. The time would come later to do that, and I was thousands of miles away to boot.

I met Juan Carlos and Jeanine at the tapas bar, and he asked how the delivery went. I told him it went fine without incident. I didn't want to give him any more details about Interpol or how strange and out of the norm the delivery was since I wasn't sure what his role was in this, if he had any at all. Jeanine looked beautiful as usual and touched my arm saying she was concerned about me. I told her I was fine and wanted to prepare for the concert at the castle so I would devote tomorrow to that. She told me only good reviews had come in from the tour and that we would have to get together and strategize about how to maximize the PR from it. I told her I looked forward to concentrating on my career more when I got back to New York. She asked me how Eve was doing, and I just said she was fine, even though I hadn't spoken to her in at least a week. Jeanine said to let her know if I needed anything and Juan Carlos seconded that. I thanked them and after sangria and a few tapas I headed back to my room. I was exhausted and could use a good night's sleep.

As I started to change there was a knock on my door. I thought, here we go again. And, of course, it was Luca outside my door. I had no choice but to let him in. As he entered, he seemed a little more well-mannered than before. He asked, "Mr. Lanbourne, how did the delivery of the package go? Did you notice anyone possibly following you or did anything out of the ordinary happen?" I said, "everything went smoothly as far as I knew but it seemed strange to me that I was let in so easily." Luca then replied, "this is not something for you to worry about, we, of course, arranged it to be that way." He then asked me for my bank account number so they could transfer the funds for my services. I asked him, "can I give that to you at a later date since I don't have the information handy?" He gave me an email address and told me to send it there. I would receive ten thousand euros for the delivery. I was a bit shocked. Ten thousand euros? What did I do that was so valuable? Obviously, something devious or they wouldn't buy me off like this. I just thanked him and said, "I'll send it along as soon as I can." He then left without incident saying again, "Do not say a word of this to anyone and act like it never happened or there could major repercussions." My thinking was I didn't want to accept money from the WTC since it might implicate me as an accomplice in what was happening.

I passed out on the bed exhausted mentally and physically. I would deal with everything tomorrow, not really knowing what the future held. Little did I know there were unexpected twists in the works for me out at the castle. And why was I performing just one piece of music? There had to be something else behind this, not just a fifteen minute performance?

CHAPTER 14

The Plot Thickens

I woke up the next morning feeling refreshed. I had slept for ten hours; I needed it. I decided to treat myself to a Spanish royal breakfast and ordered the works from room service. I needed sustenance and would treat myself well today not knowing what the future held. The food arrived and I ate like a king—Spanish potato omelet, toast with tomatoes, olive oil and jam, pastries, and of course, churros sandwiches. The coffee in Spain was so good that I indulged in multiple cups. I was extremely satisfied and needed a break before practicing so I went for a walk around the area. Being close to the hotel was a wise idea. Interpol had called me to confirm that I delivered the package as they had already surmised.

After walking around the streets of Madrid for a while I noticed the same men a couple of times, dressed in thin leather coats and staying a distance away from me. I assumed they were from Interpol, so I wasn't concerned. I went back to the room and sat down to practice *Invocation and Dance*. That was my order of the day, or so I thought. About an hour later the phone rang, it was Mario Sincenzi from Interpol. He asked me to meet him at a café around the corner from the hotel at 5pm in the afternoon. He said he had some news to tell me and wanted a secure place to do it. He said, "We have things to discuss that are of international significance." I agreed. It was two o'clock now, so I had time to practice a bit more and rest.

I met Mario at the café in a back room that apparently was a meeting place for Interpol. We sat down and he ordered espressos. Mario then went on to tell me two things, "Jonathan, there is a mole in the United States Embassy, and we have a pretty good idea who it is based on the information you gave us, but we still need more proof." The other thing was that apparently there was some connection between Senator Lee's visit and the World Trade Company. Senator Lee was about to cast a vote on the Armed Services Committee against an arms deal that the WTC was the middleman on. The arms were meant for the Middle East, and he believed they would end up in the wrong hands. Mario continued "if these weapons fall into a certain group's hands it could mean the end of a democracy in the Middle East as we know it." Senator Lee was the only no vote on the committee that would stop the deal so the package may be what they are using to prevent his vote. Mario then said, "we need you to continue in your role since there may be more to be uncovered once you reach the castle." I asked if it was really necessary since I had done what they had asked of me and my involvement was negligible at this point. He said, "we need to play out all the angles and you are one of them. More might transpire than you think, and Interpol will protect you, so you are not in harm's way." I thought, "do I really have a choice? One way or another I am involved and might as well see this through to the end, whatever that was." I agreed to continue as asked but didn't feel comfortable with my spy designation. I went back to the hotel and hit the bar again to relax—Macallan 12 time again. And to boot, I ordered one of their Spanish steaks Galician-style. I thought if the castle would be my last stand, then I would have to live well before. Maybe it was my last supper, so I had to make the most of it?

CHAPTER 15

The Castle

The next day before my concert at the castle I had breakfast again at the hotel and received a message from Jeanine that she would like to meet for lunch. As my manager, I agreed of course, because I also wasn't sure what her and Juan Carlos's involvement with this was at this point. She seemed to show up all the time all over the place. We were to meet in the hotel at 2pm in the afternoon. I said to myself this might be interesting. What was she hiding?

We met in the restaurant by the bar. She looked fabulous, of course. What was her game here? Or was I just imagining things that didn't exist? We ordered Sangria and appetizers, and she once again said she was concerned about me, that I had gotten into something I wasn't prepared to get out of. She asked if I wanted to cancel the castle concert in Segovia and just go back to New York. I said I had been looking forward to performing the Rodrigo and didn't want to cancel. She asked if I was sure and asked if it would be easier just to cancel and get back home to Eve. I told her I preferred to go through with it. She agreed, but since we had a day left before the concert, asked me to let her know if I change my mind. Then she leaned over and said, "I'm worried about you, you need to think about your safety first, but I understand the artist in you needs to perform." I replied, "this is just something I have to do, to see this tour through to the end in its entirety." Jeanine said, "if you feel this way then I can't change your mind, but please be careful and attentive to your surroundings when you're there." I thought her concern showed to me she had more involvement in this than she led on. I would find that out later.

We ate dinner and talked some more. Jeanine then asked, "would you like company in your room tonight?" She said laughingly she would be happy to relieve my anxiety and that only we would know. No one else needed to know, especially not Eve. I asked her what was going on with her and Juan Carlos. She said it wasn't serious, just a fling that she took advantage of. I told her if she wanted to come up to my room for a drink we could just talk. Sex was off the table, but I wouldn't mind the company since I was preoccupied with what was going on. She said she understood and agreed and would control herself, she promised.

We went up to the room and I ordered a bottle of wine, Sauvignon Blanc, which Jeanine liked. We talked for a while and I asked her how things were going back home with her kids. She said her mom was helping her out, so everything was fine. She asked me further how I was mentally, and I said I would get through this okay. We spoke further and I was a bit burnt from the day and the drinking, so I said I was going to bed. She said she would show herself out and speak to me tomorrow. I went to bed and passed out.

The next morning, I woke up and there was Jeanine, next to me in bed, fully clothed. I woke her up and after a bathroom break, she said she was too wiped out to go to her hotel and not to worry, nothing happened here. I said if it did, I had no recollection of it. She assured me again that nothing transpired here. She said, "Jonathan, I wished something had happened but don't worry, it didn't." She then headed for the door and said she would be in touch and hoped talking last night helped to allay my anxiety a bit. I thanked her and asked her to let me know how I will be getting to the castle tomorrow and what time I should be ready. She said she would and departed albeit wobbly.

CHAPTER 16

The Castle Continued

I was up early the next day ready to depart for the castle. I was being picked up by a limo at 4pm for an hour or so drive. There would be food and drink for me and time to meet my host who had requested me. I wasn't sure what I was doing or where this was going but I had to follow it through. After tonight I hoped to depart for New York on October 20th in the early morning. I looked to get in and out of the castle ASAP and back to the hotel. That was my plan at least.

4pm came and I was downstairs waiting for the limo. A tall, Lurch-like driver dressed in black with a cap introduced himself as Thiago and asked in a deep voice, "Mr. Lanbourne, do you have everything you need for tonight? If not, I would be happy to get anything for you." I said I'm fine and we proceeded to the limousine. As I entered the limo, I noticed there were no handles to open the doors from the inside. This was alarming. I was trapped in this car not knowing what intentions the driver had. I could check in to the limo but could not check out.

We headed out onto the highway and Thiago asked if I wanted water or something else to drink. There was a whole mini bar in the limo that opened up if I wanted it. I said maybe I would, and he opened the bar. The question was, if I had a drink now would it affect my performance? I thought it might actually help since my nerves were off the charts, so I indulged in one and only one, of course, Macallan 12 that was in the mini bar. It was as if they knew what I wanted. Were they actually following me that closely?

The ride to the castle was stunning. Rolling hillsides, ancient castles and structures, rivers, lakes and more. When we arrived, Thiago opened my door and let me out. I was relieved. The castle was a magnificent structure, my guess was it dated back a thousand years. Who lived here? My guitar and I entered the castle. Since I was performing the Rodrigo, I took the Armin Hanika guitar with me. It had a more traditional, deeper tone than my Pedro de Miguel which was meant for flamenco and more traditional Spanish repertoire. My guitar and I entered the castle together, hopefully to depart in a timely fashion. I felt like I was stepping into an abyss.

I was shown into a small room with fourteenth century tapestries lining the walls." What was I doing here," I asked myself. I unpacked and prepared myself for the upcoming performance. A servant, from what I surmised, entered the room and asked me if I wanted anything to eat or drink. I asked for some tapas and sangria so I wouldn't be hungry when I was performing. There is nothing worse than having a growling stomach during a performance. Within fifteen minutes, the food and drink were brought in. I indulged in it and warmed up and rested. I felt good and scarily intrigued by what the evening held for me. What was this all about and who was behind it?

I was led into a large space with artwork and statues and seated at what seemed to be a small stage. The floors were marble so I knew the acoustics would be incredible and that my notes would be bouncing off the ceilings. There was no audience though, who was I performing for? The mystery continued to unfold.

CHAPTER 17

The Performance

As I sat there ready to perform for whomever, a light came on in the back of the room. In walked an elderly woman dressed like a queen in an elegant gown. She looked like she could have been in any of the Spanish Royalties courts. I surmised she was in her late sixties or early seventies and once had been a very beautiful woman of the court. She carried herself royally, seemingly being born into her title. She introduced herself as the Marquesa de Segovia and the President of the World Trade Company. A chill went down my spine with those words. She said she had requested my performance since Joaquin Rodrigo was her favorite Spanish composer and the *Invocation and Dance* his most mysterious piece. The Marquesa then said, "the people who support me have one other requirement here." I couldn't imagine what that would be.

The Marquesa went on to say "Mr. Lanbourne, what will happen to you after your performance depends on how well you perform, it must be flawless, if not I cannot guarantee your safety. I know this piece very well since I have heard it performed many times. I was even privileged to meet Maestro Rodrigo on a couple of occasions." I was floored. I assumed she was talking about Luca and the likes but why would I have to perform flawlessly? How could my performance affect anything the WTC was doing unless this was just part of some warped scheme? And what was going on at the United States Embassy? I asked the Marquesa for an explanation, but she just said, "We have our reasons." I asked if I could use the bathroom before starting and she consented with a nod to the guard to go with me. In the bathroom I reached into my pocket and pulled out a flask of Macallan 12. I needed a couple of shots to calm down and get through this. I didn't want my hands to shake during the performance, so I took a couple gulps—a bad way to drink a good scotch that should be sipped! But it did the trick.

The Rodrigo starts out with a mystical section that is all harmonics that sound like distant bells with one dissonant chord in between each harmonics line. It then bursts into arpeggios and chords that clash and go in and out of dissonant and melodic lines. I started slowly and things flowed as I relaxed. My mind was solely on the performance at this point. It was as if the music was playing itself through my hands. I thought, if I am going to go out, I would go out in style, with whiskey and classical guitar.

As I proceeded through the piece, I reached the middle section which, after the smashing together of sounds of the first half, then goes into melodic dance sections. I thought

I broke into that well and was flying through it and actually enjoying myself when I got to the tremolo section which needed all the attention I could give it. I told myself to slow down and stay in control. It's too easy to make a mistake in this section with this technique since it is so demanding. I got through it well with no technical mistakes. Interpretively I felt it could have been better, but I'm not sure the Marquesa would know that.

As I careened into the last dance section before the end, I felt back in control but maybe had taken the tempo a bit too fast. On the last measure of the last dance segment, I stumbled a bit missing one of the chords. Was it noticeable? I was sure it was. What would happen now as I finished up the rest of the piece flawlessly? What crazy scheme had they cooked up?

The Marquesa stood up and all she said was, "thank you for your performance, Mr. Lanbourne." She then exited the room as I stood there motionless and thought, what the hell? Sure enough, as I stood there, in walked Luca and ordered the other guards to take me to section D of the castle. He would be along momentarily. I had expected him to show up at some point. Section D, what was that? The guards escorted me down a long hallway down a stairway that led to the basement of the castle. The guards then led me to a windowless room with a table and some visual equipment. I was told to wait there until further notice. What was to happen next was unpredictable, at least so I thought. The logic of it all escaped me.

Sergei and Luca entered the room like something out of a spy novel from the cold war era. Both dressed in dark black suits, not very stylish, with skinny ties and black shoes. Sergei asked if I wanted anything to drink, I said that depended on what happened here next. He said, "we have something very special for you" it was a bottle of Macallan 12 and a Glencairn whiskey glass. Sergei then opened it and said have a drink on us and filled the glass and pushed it towards me. For the first time in a long time, I didn't want a drink. I just wanted to get the hell out of there alive, but I felt obligated to take a drink while they studied me.

Sergei then said, "you know my associate Luca and you have seen some of what he can do, but not all of it. Therefore, we have another assignment for you due to your lack of a flawless performance tonight, as the Marquesa has said it so." I asked why I had to perform flawlessly to escape this assignment. Sergei just said, "we do what the Marquesa says, no questions asked." He then went on to say "tomorrow, you will go back to the embassy and retrieve the package. Robert Somerfield will arrange for it to be handed to you upon your arrival. Just bring it back to the hotel and wait for further instructions. If you do your part, you will be allowed to fly back to New York. If not, we will make sure you never play guitar again." I knew I had no choice but to do what they said. I was then escorted out of the castle to the limo where Thiago was waiting to bring me back to the hotel. Thiago asked, "how did your performance go, Mr. Lanbourne?" I answered, "I'm not sure, under usual circumstances it would have been considered pretty good." But these weren't normal circumstances, it was bazaar.

When I arrived back at the hotel a note had been slipped under my door. It said "Meet me at the café at 10:30pm, MS." I knew MS was Mario from Interpol and the café was the one around the corner we had met previously. My thoughts now went to what was the plan for tomorrow. My guess was that I would be picking this package up after it had already done its damage. I hoped Mario had answers for me. If he didn't, I would be in no man's land, up the creek without a paddle, or whatever cliché fit the situation for the time being.

CHAPTER 18

The Plan Continued

I arrived back at the hotel at 9:30pm and saw there was a message on my phone to meet Juan Carlos and Jeanine down at the bar for a drink. Without changing, I went downstairs since I didn't have a lot of time before meeting Mario at the café. I arrived at the bar and there sat Juan Carlos and Jeanine. The bar was basically empty, so we sat at a high-top table in an isolated corner of the room just off the bar. I ordered bottled water this time; I needed to keep my faculties clear.

Juan Carlos asked how the performance at the castle went since he wanted to report back to the European Union Cultural Council. I just answered it was okay but could have been better. I wasn't sure how much I should tell him at this point since I still wasn't sure what Juan Carlos's role was in all this. Jeanine then asked who I performed for. I said for one person only, the Marquesa de Segovia. Jeanine said how unusual that was, and I agreed. She then asked if anything else unusual happened. I just replied not really but thought that was an unusual question coming from her. I didn't want to lead on as to what they had asked me to do. I was weighing my risks and didn't want to reveal any details.

Juan Carlos excused himself from the table to make a phone call in the lobby. Jeanine then went on to say she would be flying back to New York tomorrow and asked if there was anything else she could do for me. She could help me celebrate the tour before we left. I told her thanks for the offer, but I was fine and just wanted to get up to my room to rest and would see her back in New York. When Juan Carlos returned from the lobby, I said I was tired and wanted to get back up to my room. We said our goodnights and they both congratulated me on a successful tour.

When I arrived at the café Mario was there waiting for me. Once again, we went to the back room where it was private. I told him about my performance at the castle and what had happened. Mario said, "we had no idea the Marquesa de Segovia was actually the President of the World Trade Company, but it makes sense since she has showed up in a number of their illegal dealings. This is excellent intel, Jonathan, something we couldn't confirm previously. Unfortunately, you are still going to have to follow through with what we've asked. Apparently, the CIA has been tracking the WTC and Interpol has had an investigation open on them for five years, but we have never been able to prove they were involved in covert arms deals." The intensity in Mario's speech and in his eyes showed how motivated he was to nail the WTC. I replied, "at this point, Mario, I'm too far in to stop so I'll do whatever you ask." I came to the conclusion I would never be safe again unless these people were brought to justice.

I asked Mario how they would stop the device from being triggered tomorrow and releasing the Havana Syndrome at the embassy when Senator Lee was there. He said, "since we are aware of it, we have put in place a blocking system that hopefully will stop the electronic waves from affecting anyone within its reach." I asked if Senator Lee was at risk at all since this was apparently their plan. Mario said, "Senator Lee is aware of the situation and will play along. As soon as he enters the embassy, he will be whisked to the bunker in the basement so he will be out of harm's way. There will also be a body double from Interpol dressed to look like him who will take his place." What spy novel was I in, body double?

Mario said all he wanted me to do was to pick up the device and bring it back to the hotel. There they could apprehend anyone from the WTC who retrieved it and finally have proof. He said the risk to me was minimal and they would have agents following me every step of the way. I was in a pickle again; I had to do what each side asked. I was out of options and felt like a puppet with strings attached being manipulated from both sides.

There were many *what ifs* here. What if things didn't go as planned, or if a third player emerged we didn't know about, or I am kidnapped and forced to do more for them, or worse yet killed. Heading back to my hotel, I was riddled with anxiety but out of options. It would be what it would be and it would end up however it would turn out. It was out of my control, apparently.

CHAPTER 19

The Pickup

I awoke early the next morning trying to psyche myself up for what had to be done today. After showering I went down to the lobby to have breakfast to see if I could eat anything. I decided I would call Eve and spill the beans on everything that had been going on here, so she was aware in case anything happened to me. After coffee and a quick bite, I called Eve from my room. She didn't pick up, so I left a message asking her to call me back ASAP and that it was important.

Sure enough, she called me back about twenty minutes later. I told her "I don't know where to begin but I am somehow involved in a plot to hurt or kill a United States Senator in order for a weapons deal to go through the United States Congress that would probably kill thousands of innocent people." She asked emphatically, "why is this the first I'm hearing about this since the question of delivering the package? It's not good you've kept me out of the loop." I replied, "I did not want to worry you since I thought I would deliver it, and it would be over." Men, as I can attest, are not great communicators with their significant others. At least I know I am guilty of it. I swore I would keep her in the loop going forward and now had Interpol's help.

Eve was very upset with me and the situation and said she was going to contact the authorities in New York, but I told her the CIA and Interpol were already involved so I wasn't sure what good that would do and that it might jeopardize the whole operation. She then said, "I'm getting on the next flight to Madrid and will be there in the morning." I told her, "whatever happens will be finished today so it's best you wait. By the time you get here it will be over, one way or the other." I told her, "you are the love of my life and I'm sorry I haven't kept you informed. I'm hopeful this will end up okay." I had to hang up to go to the embassy and do my part and said "Honey, if something happens to me, just know you were the best thing that ever happened to me, my one and only true love." She started to cry over the phone saying, "it is the same for me, Jonathan, I'll love you always. I will be by my phone the rest of the day and night awaiting your call." I could hear the fear and anxiety in her voice, and it tore me apart inside. I had to make this right whatever the cost!

I arrived at the embassy at around noon. The guard at the front again asked me for my passport and who I was here to see. I, of course, answered Robert Somerfield. He told me to wait until he contacted him. A minute or so later the guard instructed me to take the same walkway I did before to the back of the building and wait by the door there. I went to the door and shortly after the door opened and Robert

Somerfield was there with the package. He handed me a piece of paper and said "Deliver this to the address on the note I just handed you. Memorize it now and destroy the note immediately." I thought this was not the plan, as far as Interpol knew I was bringing it back to the hotel. The address on the note was twenty-three Amor de Dios, Madrid. I memorized it and tore the note up. My only hope was that Interpol would track my phone and follow me to the address and follow up from there. Having not heard about any attacks on the embassy today I figured the deterrent Interpol had put in place worked and the WTC wanted to get rid of the evidence. I just hoped I wouldn't end up like Jordan Long, a casualty of covert operations!

The embassy wasn't far from the street Amor de Dios so I walked along the promenade with the package trying to come up with alternate scenarios that would allow me to escape if I needed to. As I approached Amor de Dios, I noticed a black sedan parked not far from the address. The street itself was a back street that normally didn't look like it had a lot of traffic to begin with, so the sedan stood out. I couldn't imagine Interpol would be that dumb and obvious. Maybe it wasn't Interpol, maybe it was that third player? My mind was racing a hundred miles an hour it seemed.

I walked up to the door timidly and knocked. My heart was racing, and I was sweating bullets. This was worse than being onstage. At first nothing, then as I stood there the sedan took off fast and was coming straight at me. I started to run holding the package close but there was nowhere to go, no back alleys or other entrances. The sedan cut me off and forced me into a corner. The door swung open, and I heard a familiar voice say "get in fast." It was Jeanine in the back seat. I thought, "What the hell?" I jumped in and she said she would explain later but at the moment they had to get out of here. Juan Carlos was at the wheel driving. Just as she said that a black SUV rammed us from the side, but Juan Carlos was able to floor it and get around the corner as the SUV chased us through the streets of Madrid. Then I heard gunshots ring out, the sedan windows must have been bullet proof but the back door where Jeanine was had been rammed and had a large opening. I looked at her and saw she had been hit in the shoulder. She called out "Juan Carlos, call in support from Interpol," as she held her arm having been hit. Juan Carlos said he couldn't since he was trying to get away so Jeanine said, "take my phone out of my pocket and hit the pound key; that is a direct dial to Interpol and emergency notification." I did what she asked, and Juan Carlos was able to maneuver us down a street next to a river that seemed safe for the moment. Jeanine said Interpol would track her phone and be there shortly.

As we sat there waiting for help to arrive Juan Carlos was outside the car behind a door with gun in hand prepared for the black SUV. I asked Jeanine what was her involvement with all this and she said, "Juan Carlos and I work for the CIA and have been following the WTC for five years now, we have been working with Interpol to get evidence about them on weapons trafficking. We have had many opportunities that never panned out but if we could connect them to this device you were told to deliver, we could issue warrants to arrest the President and Vice President of the WTC." I could see she was in pain so I helped to put pressure on her wound until help arrived. She said she would explain further her involvement later. I didn't push the issue at that point. I was running on adrenaline now and hyper-focused on what was happening around me.

Just then, we could all see the black SUV about half a mile away racing towards us. Juan Carlos said we had no choice but to make a stand since the car was badly damaged and we couldn't get away. He looked at me and asked, "do you have any experience with a gun?" I said, "well I've been to the shooting range a couple of times just for fun, but never had to shoot at anyone." He handed me a gun and said, "we have no choice. This won't be for fun; it will be for your life." I took it and removed the safety so I could fire when needed. We watched as the SUV came closer and closer. I thought, well this is it, now I can go out guns a blazing like in the movies. Only now in real life, mine depended on it. I gripped the gun with sweaty hands and hoped I could hit the broad side of a barn if it came to that, as the saying goes.

CHAPTER 20

The Shootout

As the SUV raced towards us, I could see another black sedan racing behind it. Juan Carlos positioned me next to him and in front of Jeanine. He said, "don't fire until I give you the order and stay behind the car door that is bulletproof." I said, "I got it," hopefully. As both cars raced towards us the one behind the SUV opened fire on it. I thought they must be Interpol. It seemed though that unless they were able to slow the SUV down, they would get to us first. I thought, "I'm about to get into a shootout, what the hell? I'm supposed to be onstage playing my guitars. How did I end up here? I'll bet Segovia never had to do this in his career!"

Just as the SUV approached, it veered off onto a side street away from us seemingly to avoid the gunshots from the car chasing them. The black sedan didn't follow the SUV but continued towards us. Juan Carlos recognized the driver—it was Mario from Interpol with another agent, so he told us to stand down. The car pulled up next to us and

Mario hopped out asking how Jeanine was. Juan Carlos said we had stopped the bleeding, but she needed to get to a hospital ASAP. Mario said Jeanine and I should hop in his car, and he called for backup for Juan Carlos. Mario said he would secure the package and get it to headquarters. The only question I had was, where was the SUV hiding? My thoughts were racing at a supersonic rate. I was sure it was near.

We arrived at a nearby hospital which was about ten minutes from where we were. Jeanine didn't look so good and was in pain, but I knew she would be alright now. I told her I would wait with her to make sure she was okay. Mario then left with the package and left us with an Interpol agent guarding us. I didn't feel very secure since the SUV was out there somewhere wandering the streets of Madrid. I went to the waiting room to wait for news on Jeanine from the doctor. Apparently, she had to go into surgery to remove the bullet from her shoulder. I told the agent I was going to the men's room and he nodded. As I walked through the door of the bathroom I was grabbed by the collar and thrown against the wall. It was Luca! He said, "where is the package Mr. Lanbourne?" I told him I didn't have it anymore; Interpol had taken it. He said, "if you don't retrieve it and are lying, I will track you down and end your time on this planet." I said, "how am I supposed to retrieve it? It is out of my hands now." He responded, "find a way, Jonathan." He left saying he would be in touch soon. I knew he meant business but what could I do? I was a nervous wreck. What was I to do and how would I get the package back?

By the time I got back to the waiting room I was sure Luca was gone. He was for sure the one chasing us in the SUV. I told the Interpol agent what happened, and he ran to the bathroom to see if he could locate Luca, but he was gone. He came back and in his broken English said he had reported it to Mario, so he was aware. If Luca were able to recover the device, there would be no evidence against the WTC.

Jeanine came out of surgery about forty-five minutes later and was now in the recovery room. A nurse showed me in to see her once she woke up and she thanked me for being there and grabbed my hand. She said, "I will explain all this to you in due time, please just be patient right now." I said I understood and just wanted her to recover. She squeezed my hand hard, and I felt for her. She was a good, beautiful person. How she got involved with the CIA was a mystery to me and I guess what she had to explain later. If I didn't have Eve I could have fallen in love with her. But I was in love with my Eve and knew that wouldn't change.

The doctor came over and told us she would be kept overnight and released in the morning. I said I would let Juan Carlos know. Jeanine then grabbed my hand again and said, "You know Juan Carlos and I are not an item; it was just a cover for this job." I told her I had figured as much and would be back in the morning to help her get back to her room. She thanked me and said she probably would have to go to Interpol headquarters to be debriefed so not to worry. Juan Carlos would pick her up. I told her I would check in with her tomorrow to make sure she was okay. She pulled me over and gave me a kiss on the cheek and said, "thanks, Jonathan.

You are so sweet, and you know how I feel about you. That is not a cover, but real." I said "I know. I'm taken, but will be your friend always." I left to go back to the hotel hoping everything went well with the package and device and there were no other hitches. Of course, Luca was still out there!

CHAPTER 21
The WTC

When I got back to the hotel, it was Macallan 12 time. I was exhausted! An Interpol agent had been assigned to me, so I felt pretty safe. After an hour or so at the bar I headed upstairs to my room with the agent not far behind me. Once I got to my room I collapsed on the bed. Shortly after I heard a scuffle out in the hallway. I got up and looked in the peep hole and didn't see anything, not even the agent. I opened the door a crack to find him, and there was a boom, Luca was there and kicked the door open to the room and knocked me on my ass. He entered quickly and shut the door behind him. He said "Mr. Lanbourne, you are coming with me. Don't put up a struggle or I may have to do something that I really don't want to do at this point." I knew what he meant so had no choice but to again do as I was told. Interpol had failed me again.

He snuck me out a door downstairs in the hotel's kitchen and into a limo. Thiago of course was the driver. I was put in the back seat alone and Luca sat in the front passenger seat. I guessed I was going out to the castle again for a visit with the President of the WTC, the Marquesa de Segovia. What I could do for them at this point was unclear. I didn't have the device or access to it. Or maybe, they wanted to tie up any loose ends and get rid of me. Either way it didn't bode well for me. My whole life flashed before me and I felt bad for Eve who might become a widow. This whole thing was crazy and completely out of my world! What lay ahead was unknown and up to my captors.

We arrived at the castle, and I was locked in a small room down the stairs that looked like it could have been a prison a hundred or so years ago where prisoners were tortured. After about an hour, two guards came in and escorted me up to the room I had performed in and sat me down roughly in the chair. I knew I wasn't here to perform the Rodrigo again. A back door opened and in walked the Marquesa in her queen-like attire. This time she wasn't so polite. She said "Mr. Lanbourne, I warned you about your performance and what might happen to you. You will make a video for us with a script we will provide for you. If you do not agree to do this, we will do what is necessary." I asked what the video would say, and she just told me it was not my concern what the content was, just to do what I was told, or they would have to force it out of me. What choice did I have but to do it?

I was brought back down to the apparent dungeon and was told they would come to get me when the time came to record the video. About a half hour later I was marched into a room and sat in front of a camera and given a script. This time it was Sergei who was there and told me I must read the script as written. He said I had five minutes to read it over and that they would record it. It demanded the return of the device, or I would be executed within five hours. The exchange would be the device for me, no questions asked. I was a hostage with no real value politically. I thought, "will I get out of this alive?" The camera rolled and I read the script as asked. I started, "my name is Jonathan Lanbourne, I am currently being held hostage. My captors demand the return of their property in exchange for my life. They give you until 9pm to return the package in question, that is five hours from now, or I will be executed. They say don't test us; we will do as we said if you don't comply. Once the exchange is agreed upon, details will be provided." When I finished, my hands were shaking uncontrollably. My life may be over I thought, and I have really just begun to live. I swore to myself if I got out of this alive, I would live the rest of my life to the fullest with no regrets. Everything would be on the table, no excuses. I would live in the moment, not knowing what comes next! I just hoped I would have the opportunity to do just that.

CHAPTER 22

The Exchange

I was brought back down to the dungeon and told to wait. It would be a few hours before they heard anything. I knew the castle was well guarded behind multiple layers of entry so a rescue attempt wouldn't happen. I ran scenarios over and over in my head to see what, if any, possibilities there were. Time went by slowly and I didn't have a watch on, so I had no idea what time it was. All I knew was these five hours might be my last.

As we got closer to 9pm, I expected someone to come and get me at any moment. Sure enough, I heard footsteps approaching. Two guards came to get me, unlocking the door and dragging me upstairs. I asked what was happening but neither responded. I was returned to the chair in the room where I performed, and the Marquesa was there with Sergei. Sergei said "Interpol has agreed to the exchange; you will be taken out in a van to a location by the river for the exchange and please, Mr. Lanbourne, no shenanigans!" I was relieved but concerned. What if something went wrong, would I be safe? There were no answers to the many questions I had, I just had to hope for the best.

They tied my hands in front of me and put me in the back of a black van. As Thiago placed me in the back seat he said quietly in my ear "When I say run, run!" Was he working with Interpol? When we headed out to the location at a high speed, I could see what looked like Thiago at the wheel driving. Sergei and the two guards entered the car after I was placed in the back seat and were in the back with me. In Spanish he told them the procedure. I could understand most of it since I knew a bit of the language having communicated with so many Spanish musicians. As we got to the location, Sergei told them to take up positions on the high ridges. They both had long-range sniper rifles and looked like they knew how to use them.

Sergei grabbed me by the arm and walked me out in front of the van. Reckoning time had come. I could see a car straight ahead that looked like the one Mario was in during the river chase. Sergei called out for them to bring the package over and place it halfway between us and them. One of their men would retrieve it and verify it was the device and after that they would release me. Mario responded, "how do we know you will release the prisoner?" Sergei responded "You don't, but this is the way it must go down if you want him back. We have no quarrel with him." What I didn't know that I found out later, was that the WTC had a private jet waiting for them at a small private airport to escape once they had the package in hand. The Marquesa, Sergei, Robert

Somerfield, and Luca would be on that plane on its way out of the country to an undisclosed country in the Middle East. Without the device, Interpol's evidence against them would be sketchy at best and just one person's word against the others.

As a member of Interpol brought the package halfway to us, out of the corner of my eye I saw Thiago starting to edge closer to Sergei. I was hoping all those days on the treadmill and running up the Hudson River path would serve me well now. Although it would have helped to have Nikes on. Suddenly Thiago lunged at Sergei and pushed him to the ground. He yelled at me to run! Luca then fired at me as I ran. I could hear a bullet fly by my right ear. I veered off down the river where I was not exposed and took cover. I wasn't sure what had happened back there to the package and where it stood now so I continued to run. I just knew I ran like hell to get out of there. My heart was pumping away at a hundred miles an hour and I was short of breath; I was running for my life literally. I thought "I really need to get into better shape."

I decided to work my way down the riverbank and just kept going to get as far away as possible. I finally worked my way back onto a walkway and could see no one around so I ran to a corner and hailed a taxi. I went back to the hotel but didn't go right to my room since I thought if things went south back there someone might be waiting for me. As I entered the hotel cautiously, I was grabbed by the arm. It was Juan Carlos. He shuffled me to a secure location in the hotel and said, "just follow me quickly, you need to come with me now." I did as he asked. We got into the black sedan and sped off. He said, "we are going to Interpol's headquarters; we need to debrief you on everything that has happened and make sure you will be safe moving forward." I said I would go. Did I have a choice? Juan Carlos and Jeanine, CIA agents, jeez, I didn't see that one coming.

Back at Interpol headquarters I was brought into a room. Mario came in and said he would need to record our conversation, so it was on the record. I said of course, I had nothing to hide. He went through the whole history of what had transpired since I was contacted by the WTC. He asked me questions to verify everything. As he spoke, I added more information so the recounting of what went down was correct. What I found out was that Robert Somerfield was working with the WTC for a very high price. Being the United States Assistant Ambassador to Spain in Madrid, he had access to whatever they needed. I was just a pawn in the game, an unsuspecting delivery man to be used. It seemed obvious but still escaped me why they chose me?

I asked Mario what happened at the exchange, and he said because I had escaped, they were able to quickly recover the package. Thiago had been working for Interpol and was wounded in the shootout. He was currently hospitalized. I asked if I could send him my thanks for saving me and Mario said that when the time was right I could. Right now, there were other loose ends. Sergei and Luca had escaped, and Interpol had tracked them; they were headed for an airport just outside Madrid. Mario said they were hoping to apprehend them before takeoff. Hopefully that would be so because if they got away, I might not be safe anywhere since revenge is a very strong motive with these people. I hoped Interpol would catch them and put an end to this chapter of my life. But who knew if it would ever end? I knew three things about the way things went down, I survived the exchange, I would see Eve again, and I would play guitar again. These were very comforting to me right now as I found out the details of what happened. You never know how things will turn out when the crap hits the fan. Luckily, I had people looking out for me, for the most part.

CHAPTER 23

The Chase

This is how the airport scene went down according to Mario. The CIA, led by Juan Carlos, had intervened on the part of Interpol. Having special forces troops in the area, they called them in to stop the flight of the WTC jet. As Luca, Sergei, Robert Somerfield, and the Marquesa boarded the plane, the troops surrounded it and gave them an ultimatum of having to breach the plane if they didn't come out voluntarily. Having no other choice, they gave themselves up. It seemed I would not have to worry about any retaliation from them, for now. I would have to be a witness though so that worried me. But what could I do? It was my ticket out of Europe. I made my statement with the understanding I could be called back at any point to testify and had to sign a document as such. For now, it seemed it was over, at least I thought it was.

The whole thing had been about an arms deal that would upset the balance of power in the Middle East. Senator Lee was against it and rightfully so. I had helped to thwart it and felt proud of that. Now it was time to get back to the hotel and pack for my flight out tomorrow. It was important to me that I get back to my art and some form of normality in my life. I would call Eve and tell her everything that had happened, sure she would be relieved. The universe had protected me from harm, and I was grateful.

When I returned to the hotel there was a message from Jeanine to meet her down at the bar at 5pm in the afternoon. I packed my things so I wouldn't have to do it later. My flight was at 10am the next morning out of Madrid. I went down to the bar and Jeanine and Juan Carlos were there talking. They greeted me warmly; Jeanine's right arm was in a sling to limit her movement. After the cheek-to-cheek greetings I asked her how she felt. She said, "it's not bad, pain killers and alcohol do amazing things." Juan Carlos said the mission was a success and thanked me for playing along with the whole thing so they could recover the device and arrest those responsible. He said he could only tell me so much about where the weapons were going but that they were meant to annihilate another country and change the balance of power in the Middle East. Only Senator Lee, the CIA, and Interpol saw through what was going on. He said when I return to the US, Senator Lee would like to meet me to thank me for saving what might possibly have been his life. I said, "I'm no hero, I was roped into this and didn't have a choice." Jeanine then said that may have been true, but that I didn't fold under pressure. I told her getting up and performing in front of two thousand people is pressure; this was nothing. We all laughed. Juan Carlos said, "I don't know if I could perform as well with someone holding a gun to my head." I just replied, "I guess Jeanine trained me well." Juan Carlos replied, "I'm sure she did." Jeanine blushed like a schoolgirl. She then diverted the conversation and said that as my manager we would debrief back in the states. I asked if it would be a CIA interrogation, and we laughed once again. She said she would tell me how she got recruited to be an agent. Maybe I will be next? Little did I know anything was possible.

I called Eve that night and told her I was fine and would tell her the whole story when I returned. She said she hadn't slept a wink since this started and would have the bottle of Macallan 12 ready for me when I returned so we could celebrate a successful tour and returning alive. I told her I couldn't wait to be with her and put all this behind us! She asked about Jeanine; I told her that she was not only my manager but a CIA operative. Eve was floored and said emphatically "What? You've got to be kidding me!" I said, "it's true, believe it or not. The single mom can not only handle an artist's management and children, but she is also a spy." We both broke out laughing hysterically. I told Eve I loved her and was going to get some rest and would see her tomorrow. She replied, "Jonathan, I thought I lost you for a moment there." I replied, "Eve, you'll never lose me, it won't be that easy to get rid of me." We both laughed and said our goodbyes until tomorrow. Better days were ahead for us, and I was looking forward to it.

CHAPTER 24

Back Home

As I boarded United Airlines flight 51 back to New York I saw a man who looked familiar. I couldn't place him but thought I knew him for sure. I was flying first class. I had upgraded my seat thinking I deserved the treat. My guitars were secure in travel cases in the baggage area, so I was ready to get out of Spain. We took off, and as I dozed off, I realized who the man I saw was. He was one of the guards at the castle that escorted me back and forth upstairs. I thought, this couldn't be a coincidence. Why wasn't he in custody? I thought, "I need to come up with a plan if this man approaches me." Panic set in as I thought what was his plan.

About halfway through the flight, four hours in, I looked back to where I had seen him sitting and the seat was empty. I tried not to lose it but with what had happened, I knew anything was possible. I kept telling myself, "okay Jon, you've come this far, everything will be okay." About thirty minutes later I looked up from my seat and the man was standing over me. He leaned down and said, "Mr. Lanbourne, you will walk with me off the plane. The arms of the WTC reach far and wide and you will be my ticket into the United States." Here I was again, in a position where I had no choice but to do what he said. We were in a confined area with nowhere to go. I said "okay, just don't hurt me." He just stared back at me and said, "you will tell the customs officer I am your cousin visiting you, do you understand?" I replied a simple "yes."

Needless to say, the rest of the trip was very stressful. What would happen when I got off the plane? Would I be whisked off somewhere never to be seen again? As we landed, I contemplated my options. Should I try and escape? We landed and as I stood up, there he was. He had no baggage apparently. We waited fifteen or twenty minutes or so to deboard and as we walked off, he held his arm under my elbow to make sure I didn't make a break for it. We walked down the long walkway and finally to customs where we stood in line together. When we got to the customs officer, he asked, "how are the two of you related?" The man told him he was my cousin from Spain, I just shook my head in agreement. The officer looked at him suspiciously and said, "we have no record of the two of you traveling together or being related, please stand aside while we confirm with Homeland Security, we will get back to you momentarily." Apparently, it had raised a red flag after what happened in Madrid and my assailant was nervous and sweating profusely—an obvious sign that he was lying, the officer surmised. I was feeling anxious, hoping help would arrive before he could do any harm. He had nothing to lose.

We started to walk to a holding area escorted by another officer when suddenly two agents approached us with their hands on their holstered guns. I said to myself this was it, something else would finally happen and I would not survive. I felt this was my reckoning—an airport gun battle or whatever. The two agents were both large and muscular and one of them said, "Mr. Lanbourne, please step aside slowly." They then ordered my captor to go onto his hands and knees. Since it seemed he didn't have a weapon I thought, as he wouldn't have been able to get it through security, he had no choice but to do what they asked. Suddenly, he rose and jumped at me with a knife he had managed to smuggle somehow onto the plane. One of the agents was quick enough to subdue him before he reached me and forced my assailant onto the ground with his whole-body weight. Another close call, how was he able to secure a knife on the flight I thought? When I asked the agents one of them said that would have to be investigated, there was a breakdown somewhere apparently.

They then whisked me away to another holding room. I was a mess emotionally. An attempt had been made on my life again. Luckily, I survived. A man entered and showed me his badge. His name was Lachlin Morrisey, and he worked for Homeland Security. He said they had been alerted by Interpol to be on alert for a suspect who fit the description of this man who came off the plane with me. Once they got to customs it set everything in motion to apprehend him. I asked him what more he knew and if I was in any danger in New York at this point. He said he didn't think so and gave me his card. He said "call me if you see anything suspicious or feel threatened. This is a matter of national security, so we must be vigilant." I thanked him as he released me to go with an agent who would help me with my bags and see me out to the baggage area. As I walked away, I felt uneasy about being able to be protected from any personal threats. I hoped what Lachlin said was true and not just some line they say to all innocent participants and informers when it comes to criminal activities.

I finally arrived home and hugged Eve. It didn't seem this day would ever come, and it didn't come fast enough. She said, "you must be exhausted; do you want to take a nap before we speak?" I said no I was fine; I'll just clean up so we can sit on the couch and catch up. I didn't know where I would begin with what happened even with the latest airport incident. I cleaned up, changed clothes, and proceeded to the living room where Eve was waiting with my glass of Macallan 12 ready. It was now late October; I had left in the beginning of September for the tour. I came back a different man. Also, one with a personal guard that had been assigned to me!

I explained to Eve everything that had happened chronologically and where I stood today, even with the incident at the airport. She was concerned about our security, and I said the agent from Homeland Security said he didn't think we were in danger and to contact him if I saw anything suspicious. He also said they would station an agent outside our building and another to follow me around for at least a month until things died down. I said, "honey, do you think I will let anything happen to us after what we've been through? I will make it my mission to secure our safety above all, even if I must hire private bodyguards." I felt suspicious of it all but told Eve I did currently feel secure in the way Homeland Security was prepared and apprehended the WTC suspect when he got off the plane. She voiced concern but said she trusted my gut judgements and explanation. I also said I would speak to Jeanine about it since she works for the CIA as well. Maybe she could help?

We sat on the couch cuddling and enjoying our drinks by our fireplace and I said to Eve, "I need to make love to you." We needed to reconnect and that was how I knew how. She was always receptive to my advances, never saying no, so we went to the bedroom. I was seeing double at that point but knew this was the way to start the healing process from the trauma of what had transpired on the tour. We dove into each other's arms and after making passionate love fell into a deep sleep. I wondered what tomorrow would be like as I faded away into slumber. I thought "what kind of person will I be when I awake after what I went through?" Only time would tell.

CHAPTER 25

Normality

I got up the next morning, rolled out of bed to my morning coffee and to my computer to check my emails. Eve said she had to go into the office for a meeting and then would come home. I looked forward to a calm dinner with her and a movie at home. I called Andrew Sisley to see how things were going at the University. He said he heard my tour was wildly successful and was glad I was back. I asked him where he heard about it, and he said Jeanine had called looking for me and she told him about it. I was sure she left out a lot. I told Andrew I would head over for a bit today to get my feet back on the ground here and catch up on some paperwork that I was sure was waiting for me.

As we headed into 2019, I wondered if what happened in Europe would ever come back to haunt me. Luckily, I came out of it unharmed physically, but the mental scars would take a long time to heal. I was constantly looking over my shoulder with paranoia. Being held at gunpoint does that to one's psyche. I went over to my office at Manhattan University and sat at my desk looking at some of the paperwork there. I thought I needed a day off when Andrew entered and asked if I could come to listen to one of his students who was performing later in the week. Andrew said, "any pointers you could give him would be great so feel free." I said sure, why not. Guitar was my life, as were the people who made up the community of guitarists and musicians. It was a good feeling to be back in this world.

I sat in the small recital hall where Andrew had brought the student. He was a sophomore, 19 years old, named Joshua Feinstein, and was tall and nerdy. He announced, "I will be performing Rodrigo's *Invocation and Dance.*" I thought, how appropriate, jeez. As he began to play, I was brought back to that evening at the castle and my performance. I felt anxious but also proud of what I was able to achieve, surviving the ordeal. The music prevailed, I felt, above all. When Joshua reached the end, he looked up at me. I told him it was very good but would also offer some suggestions. I said let me demonstrate for you. As he handed me his guitar and I placed it in my lap and positioned my hands to play, I thought, "this is how it is supposed to be, the music, the guitar, and a chance to relive life every time I perform. The rest was just static and noise and needed to be shut out."

I returned home to dinner and a quiet night with Eve. And, with my visit to the university, normality had returned to my life in a more profound way. I was glad to have it back and realized now more than ever how lucky I was! My world was one of creativity and beauty unlike much of the rest of the world. I was grateful to be back in it and now viewed the world and my life in a more profound way. My outlook on life had changed, Carpe Diem, enjoy every moment! That was my mantra now.

CHAPTER 26

European Epilogue

Fast forwarding to the fall of 2023, the last five years have been the best of my life, with numerous recitals both in the United States and overseas, and a very healthy guitar department at Manhattan University. The 2018 tour had bolstered my career, and many recital requests came in from it. Eve and I have spent a lot of time together and have traveled extensively to various parts of the world, just enjoying life. Jeanine, the CIA agent, is still my manager somehow. How she is able to do all that is a mystery to me to this day. But that's Jeanine.

That being said, I can't help but wonder if I am still on anyone's radar regarding what went down five years ago. In the winter of 2019, I testified remotely against the World Trade Company giving testimony as to my part in what had happened and what transpired. Where were Luca, Sergei, and the Marchesa kept and when would they be released from imprisonment? They were all convicted of arms trafficking and other international crimes. The one thing that couldn't be proven was connecting them to the murder of Jordan Long. This concerned me because their sentences were not as long as they could have been due to the lack of their connection to it. Luca got the longest sentence of fifteen years since he was the one trying to shoot and murder everyone, while Sergei and the Marquesa only received ten-year sentences.

One thing I did learn from this was to take each day as a gift and appreciate what I have. I fell in love with the classical guitar as a teenager when hearing it for the first time at my friend's house. His sister was studying, and she was practicing Bach. The moment I heard it I was enthralled and knew what I wanted to do with my life. I would use it for good to make the world a better place. Maybe that is why this whole ordeal happened? I thwarted an attempt to harm thousands of innocent people. Nothing good ever comes from negativity and there are people in this world who will look to use others for their own gain in life. I decided to ignore those who do and be on the side of positivity in all ways, both for myself and for others, whom I could help to be the best they could be. The best I could do is be free and live life one day at a time with no strings attached!

SECOND MOVEMENT:

SOUTH AMERICA

CHAPTER 1

Fast Forward 2024

It was fall, 2024, actually, I remember the date: September 24th. There I was at my desk at the university and the phone rang, it was Jeanine. The conversation went like this, "hi Jonathan, I know you are not going to believe this, and it will seem like Deja-vu but I just received a call from the South American Cultural Council, they said they heard about your tour of Europe and would like to book you on a five country tour of South America. I said before I asked for any details, I would have to take this up with you because of what happened before. So, I ask, how do you feel about this? It would be great for your career as a next step." I asked, "what countries and cities are they asking about?" Jeanine responded "the countries would be Venezuela, Columbia, Peru, Brazil and Argentina. We didn't go into what cities in these countries but that we can follow up on if you want me to move forward on this." I asked, "when would this be?" she responded, "sometime in the spring of 2025."

I knew that parts of South America had produced some of the greatest classical guitarists and guitarists of all styles in the world so the chance to expand my reputation in that part of the world would be very tempting and as usual, Jeanine was right about it being the next step in my career. The timing was interesting though. Usually, these things are booked years in advance. I guessed I would find out more in the details to come.

I responded to Jeanine "why don't you go ahead and get more details while I discuss it with Eve, if she is onboard, I'll commit to it." Jeanine said she would do just that and we could touch base next week. I thought to myself, "here we go again, but what could possibly happen?" And so it was that my South American adventure began. Who knew what would await me there? But I knew I couldn't stay locked up in New York City too long for the rest of my career. I had to get out there again at some point. And why not now? It was as good a time as any.

CHAPTER 2

The Tour

After a lengthy serious discussion with Eve, we determined I would give it a shot and agreed to do the tour. I phoned Jeanine and told her we had discussed it, and we would do the tour if my safety could be guaranteed. Jeanine would have to pull in some CIA favors to make sure that happened. She said she would get back to me about the details in a day or so. The other caveat which I hadn't told Jeanine yet was that Eve insists on coming with me. She is the more pragmatic of the two of us so I agreed but hoped I could persuade her not to come for safety reasons. In our discussion Eve said "Jonathan, you are not going anywhere for over a month in a strange part of the world without me along. I need to keep an eye on you to keep you out of trouble." I knew I had no choice, when Eve wanted to do something its useless to argue, the writing was on the wall.

And so it went, Jeanine called back, and I told her Eve was coming too. Jeanine asked "do you think that is wise?"

I responded, "she won't have it any other way, so if I want to stay married, she is coming." Jeanine of course agreed and said she would step up the plans to have us protected and would get back with details. As far as the tour goes, the dates would be set from May 1 through June 1, 2025. I also asked her why the council chose me on such short notice and she responded another guitarist had dropped out of the tour due to health issues. Having heard of my European tour they thought I would be the perfect replacement. I said that sounded reasonable. Jeanine said, "I have to go now, dates and cities to come."

I started to choose my program in my head and thought about some of the great South American guitar composers. Heitor Villa-Lobos from Brazil and Antonio Lauro from Venezuela would have to be included, and I'd have to do further research to make it more interesting. I would start working on it tomorrow and have it finished by the end of the week so I could start practicing it. Many of the pieces I had performed before, but I wanted to choose a couple of new pieces to add to my repertoire.

The next day Jeanine called back with more details. She said "the tour will start in Caracas, Venezuela, then go to Bogota, Columbia, then on to Lima, Peru, next Rio de Janeiro, Brazil, and finish up in Buenos Aires, Argentina. There would be only one recital at a hall in each city and I would only have one representative from the South American Cultural Council who would travel around with us and make all the arrangements in each city. The representative's name would be provided to us shortly." I answered sounds good and asked

Jeanine when they needed program information. She said within the month would be fine.

So it was my South American adventure began. I hoped I could just be a musician and not anything else. Only time and circumstances would tell.

CHAPTER 3

The Program

As the tour approached, I knew I had to work out some minor arrangements to make sure everything went smoothly. Once again, Andrew Sisley, my right hand, would watch over the department. He knew I was just a text or phone call away anywhere I go so could reach me if necessary. Next was the program I had worked out by November 1st.

My program, which I sent into the South American Cultural Council, was listed as Jonathan Lanbourne, Classical Guitarist, and would consist of the following repertoire:

Two pieces (Allemande and Galliard) by John Dowland

Variations on a Theme of Mozart by Fernando Sor

Cinq Preludes by Heitor Villa-Lobos

Suite Venezolana by Antonio Lauro

Five Bagatelles by William Walton

Venezuelan Waltz by Antonio Lauro (encore piece)

Other pieces subject to addition. One guitar would be used for the performances *

*2012 Felipe Conde from Spain, classical guitar with spruce top and Indian Rosewood sides and back to be used for all repertoire

I knew the program I had chosen was very ambitious and I would have to work hard to get it up to performance level. But I had performed almost all of these before except for Suite Venezolana by Lauro. That would take some work since it is a four-movement suite. I felt comfortable with the program since it combined a few different time eras and types of music both traditional and modern and a healthy dosage of South American Music. The Walton had some Latin influences in it as well. I was sure it would be interesting to the audience since it had something for everyone who has an interest in classical guitar.

I sent the program in to Jeanine, and she said she would forward it to the council and that she was still waiting to hear who our representative would be. I asked her as soon as possible to let me know. She said of course she would.

CHAPTER 4

The Representative

It was now close to Thanksgiving 2024 when Jeanine called me and said she had been contacted by the council representative and he wanted to have a video call meeting with us as soon as possible. His name was Enrique Torroba, and he was originally from Spain but now living in Venezuela. I asked her to set it up the week after Thanksgiving so it wouldn't interfere with the holiday. She said she would get back to me once she had a day and time. Since Venezuela is in the same time zone as we are I knew it would not be a problem setting it up,

Thanksgiving came and went, and our video meeting was set up for Thursday morning of the next week, I was looking forward to speaking with Enrique Torroba to get the lowdown on the tour. Jeanine and I took the call together in my office. Enrique came on and introduced himself saying, "it is a pleasure to meet you Jonathan, I have been a fan of yours since the European tour having watched many of your videos. Coming from Spain I am a classical guitarist enthusiast who dabbles in the instrument. I assure you it will be a great tour. Do you have any questions for me?" I had a list prepared as to the logistics of the tour and compensation and proceeded to ask away. Jeanine had looked over the contract and told me most of it, I was getting paid twenty thousand dollars to do the tour with all expenses paid. After my questions Enrique added "if the tour does well attendance wise you could receive up to an additional ten thousand dollars, of course all dependent on ticket sales. We also will ask you to do some press appearances to help. I will be there to interpret if needed." I responded "wonderful, please let me know about the marketing plans for this tour, maybe I can assist in some way to get the word out in each city." Enrique said he would be back to us with more details shortly.

From what I could surmise from the video call, Enrique was in his fifties or so with thinning hair but a handsome face. He looked tall but of course it's hard to tell on the video screen. He had an accent that seemed to cross a few different cultures. Probably from living in Venezuela, he didn't have a typical Spanish accent. His English was excellent, so he was probably well schooled. We would find out more as time went on.

After the meeting was over Jeanine said to me, "I have set up through my contacts to have you and Eve escorted on the tour. One thing you must know is because of this your movements may be limited but I was told they would do what they could to allow you to see each city." I told her "thanks so much, and of course I understand and we would prefer it that way." She then asked me if I would like to have lunch with her so we could catch up personally. I told her I'd have to take a raincheck since I must teach so we agreed to meet another time. I wasn't sure if she still had feelings for me since I knew she was dating a wall street executive, I was happy for that and thought then the coast is clear for us to lunch together at a later date.

It was time to get on with the tour since 2025 was upon us. I was excited and psyched for a new adventure. It didn't turn out exactly as I thought as I would find out.

CHAPTER 4

Caracas

April 30, 2025 came and Eve and I were on a plane to Simon Bolivar International Airport in Caracas, Venezuela. It was a very long flight and we were to land the next day and be escorted to the Hotel de Nationale in the center of the city. I would be performing on May 4th at the Centro Nacional de Acción Social por la Música, one of the great concert halls in South America. I had to recover from the flight, get some good food into my system, and do some preparation and practicing for the recital.

Once settled down in the hotel, Eve and I went downstairs to the restaurant for a good meal and some down time. We would explore the city a bit tomorrow but for now it was recovery time and of course for me, McCallum 12 time. Eve, being a wine drinker, ordered a local white wine from Venezuela and we spoke about the upcoming tour some more. Enrique Torroba was to join us for dinner tomorrow night in a restaurant that he booked and loved to go to. I thought it would be interesting to pick his brain a bit and see how he got involved with the South American Cultural Council. We really didn't know anything about his background.

The next morning Eve and I headed out to see some of the city, of course accompanied by our Agency escorts, or so I thought. I wasn't sure how Jeanine had arranged it and whether they were private contractors or not but was sure glad to have them along. They basically kept their distance, so we felt pretty comfortable about the arrangement. We ventured over to The Museum of Contemporary Art of Caracas that is considered one of the most important in South America. Not having been to South America before it was a nice beginning.

After the museum Eve and I went to have Arepa's for lunch. The Arepa is the crown jewel of Venezuelan cuisine. They are golden, cornmeal patties that are a canvas for a world of flavors, filled with a symphony of ingredients like succulent shredded beef, creamy cheese, or savory black beans. It was a great lunch to have in Caracas! After that we headed back to the hotel to rest a bit before dinner with Enrique at 7pm. I also wanted to do a bit more practice to prepare.

Upon arriving back at the hotel Eve decided it was time to do something else. Before I knew it, I was naked in bed making passionate love with her, she said it would relax me. It sure did, I fell asleep for a couple hours and after that, got up just in time to do some practicing before getting ready for dinner. It was a great first day, so far! We had christened the tour.

Enrique had requested that we meet him at 6pm in the lobby so he could take us on a mini tour of the city before dinner. As we entered the lobby a tall gentleman in a chauffeur's uniform met us and said, "Enrique Torroba has asked me to escort you to our limousine, he awaits you there." I thought that was a bit unusual but went along with it. Out of the corner of my eye I saw our escorts following along so thought it wasn't a problem. The limo driver opened the door and we both got in and sure enough there was Enrique, with an open bar in the back of course. He said "it is great to meet you both in person, Jonathan I prepared a drink for you, McCallum 12 Sherry Oak, I learned it is your favorite. Senora, may I get you a drink?" Eve just responded she was fine for now and thanked him. And off we went to see some more of the city and have dinner.

After a quick tour of some of the sights in Caracas we headed over to a five-star restaurant called *Mola* that Enrique loved. It is known as "The best Mediterranean Spanish Experience in Caracas" the Michelin guide says. We entered and were escorted by the hostess to a private room that Enrique had booked where we were seated. We were also joined by a younger beautiful Venezuelan woman named Carmen that he invited to join us. I was later to find out this was just one of many for Enrique. It seemed a girl in each city for him. I asked him "how did you come to be involved with the Council?" Enrique went on, "when I lived in Spain, I was a cultural attaché for the Spanish Consulate and was relocated here to Caracas. At one point I was asked by Juan de la Rosa, the head of the Council, if I would like to come on board as an event and tour administrator for South America. I decided this was my chance to expand my influence and have more of an impact on culture throughout this continent. The arts and culture are what I love so I jumped at the chance." I said, "well I'm glad to have someone of your interest and experience guiding me over here since we are newbies here. He just answered, "it is my honor, Jonathan."

Enrique went on to order a variety of dishes and fine wines for the table and we just went along with it taking it all in. He then asked Eve, "Senora is there anything you would like to do here in South America that I can assist with?" Eve went on to say, "I would love to get out to the countryside to see how people live here, being a marketing director, I'm always interested in what the general public is interested in and here I'm not sure of that." Enrique went on "I will make that happen when the time comes. I'm sure it won't be a problem to arrange." Eve then went on to ask Carmen "how do you like living in Caracas." Carmen, who spoke excellent English, looked around thirty years old and has a voluptuous body that reminded me of Salma Hayek, answered "I love Caracas but travel to much of South America, as a matter of fact, I will be your stewardess on the private charter plane that will take you to each city. Please feel free to let me know how I can make your trip more comfortable at any time. I am at your service." Eve just looked at me, I knew what she was thinking. I could read her mind "Jonathan behave yourself!" I guess I was guilty of staring too much at Carmen. After all, she is a beautiful Latin woman and I'm a red-blooded man. But Eve always keeps me in line and out of trouble, luckily.

After dessert Enrique ran us back to the hotel saying, "I don't want to keep you up too late Jonathan, you need your rest for Sunday's performance." We thanked him and I asked Eve if she was up for a nightcap at the bar and she said "sure." As we sat down in the hotel bar, I noticed someone I had seen at the restaurant and was now here in our hotel. He didn't look like one of our escorts and just wrote it off as a coincidence. Eve then said to me, "you see that man sitting at two o'clock across from us? Wasn't he at the restaurant? I said yes, you mean the short, dark skinned muscular man, I saw him too. Nothing gets by Eve it seems when her antennae is raised. She said, "do you think he is part of our coverage team?" I said I wasn't sure if they replaced anyone, but he wasn't with us before. She just went on to say "maybe I'm paranoid but we need to keep our eyes and ears open being in a foreign country. Sometimes Americans aren't welcome." I agreed and we both had a drink and headed upstairs. Tomorrow, I would go to the concert hall and try out the stage and acoustics. I looked forward to that!

CHAPTER 5

First Performance

Centro Nacional de Acción Social por la Música was an old beautiful concert hall built in the 1930's. After some recent renovations the acoustics were wonderful. The notes bounced off the walls and resounded to all ends of the hall as I was told by Eve who listened to my rehearsal the day before. I was about to walk out onstage and get the party started to what appeared to be about a three-quarter full house. Since the hall was a large one, I thought that to be a pretty good turnout for my first recital.

My heart was racing, and I knew I had to calm down, so I took a minute to do some deep breathing exercises I had learnt. It seemed to work as I walked out, bowed to the audience, sat down and began to play. The two John Dowland pieces went okay since I was just settling down and after that dove into the *Variations on a Theme of Mozart by Fernando Sor* rather well. Then came the preludes by Heitor Villa-Lobos which always seemed to be crowd pleasers. That concluded my first half. As I walked out onstage for the second half, I saw Enrique and Carmen in the second row to my left. I hadn't noticed them before but maybe they came in late. Off I went into the *Suite Venezolana* by Antonio Lauro that I was performing for the first time. Once getting past the opening prelude the other three movements went better than I expected. I felt good going into my most challenging pieces, the *Five Bagatelles by William Walton*. They were amongst my most favorite music but the first and fifth bagatelles were extremely difficult to pull off. They were originally written for Julian Bream, one of the greatest guitarists in its history, so I knew they would be a challenge. I got through them okay with the goal to improve their performance at every tour stop. The crowd called me out for an encore, and I obliged by playing Lauro's Venezuelan Waltz which is always a crowd pleaser. All in all, I would give my performance a B and would look to improve on it as time went on. The first performance in a tour is always the hardest.

After the recital Enrique and Carmen came backstage to my dressing room and asked Eve and I to come out to celebrate. I told them I would like to get back to the hotel to drop my guitar and freshen up and we agreed to meet there in one hour. The hotel was about fifteen minutes from the hall, and we would be escorted back there of course.

We went to a small bar near the hotel, it was about 10pm and I felt good. Enrique bought drinks and appetizers for all, and we spoke about the recital. "Jonathan, how do you think it went tonight? Knowing you are a perfectionist artist I am curious to know your assessment" Enrique asked. I told him

"I think it was okay, not my best work but still passable. I assure you my best is yet to come on this tour, so I am looking forward to the rest if it." He then said he would report back to the council and let them know it was a successful first performance. Carmen then reminded us that we were to be picked up at the hotel by limo at 10am to go to a small airport nearby to fly to our next destination Bogota, Columbia by private charter jet.

We parted ways at that point and as we walked out of the restaurant saw that same short muscular man who seemed to be following us. I said to Eve "we need to find out who that is and if he is on our side?" She agreed and said, "you should reach out to Jeanine to see if our escorts are rotating or not and let her know?" I told her I would do that first thing in the morning.

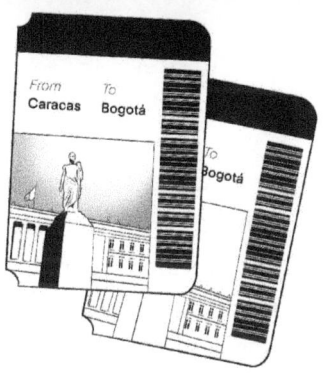

CHAPTER 6

Bogota

The private jet charter we were on was a treat for Eve and me. We were treated like movie stars being flown around South America first class. It was the way to go, no more commercial flights and having Carmen on board to attend to us wasn't a bad thing too although I wasn't sure how Eve felt about it. They seemed to hit it off a bit though since Eve can be very personable and curious and asked Carmen many questions about where we were going. As we landed, I was interested in what Jeanine would find out about the man who is following us. I asked her about the rotation and described him to her and told her he showed up wherever we were it seems. Jeanine said she would get back to me once she had some information.

Once again, a limousine picked us up and drove us to the Hotel Centro in Bogota. Another five star hotel that we were being treated to. I was to perform on May 10th at Lourdes Music Hall, another older hall in Bogota that I would look forward to seeing. In addition, I had been asked to do an interview the next morning with the classical radio station there. Enrique would come along as my interpreter, so I was happy to do it. We settled in at the hotel and I sat down to practice for an hour. The flight was short and since we flew in style, I wasn't tired from the trip. Today we would dine in the hotel just to keep things simple.

The following morning after the radio interview, we headed out to see a bit of Bogota. I still hadn't heard back from Jeanine so was curious what was going on there? We wanted to see some of the monuments in Bogota such as the Simon Bolivar statue and the bust of Evita Peron. Also, we wanted to have a typical Columbian lunch, the Ajiaco that is known as Bogota's famous signature dish. We found a small café to eat. Ajiaco is as much a part of the Bogota experience as the city's churches and mountains we were told by our concierge in the hotel. We had our two escorts along and neither one of them was the man we had seen numerous times in Caracas. We were wondering now if we were just being overly paranoid. But better safe than sorry, I guess. After my last tour I discovered you can't be too cautious.

We returned to the hotel around 4pm and were given a note to meet Enrique for dinner around the corner from the hotel at 7pm. The restaurant was called Sabores de Bogotá (Tastes of Bogota), a fairly common Columbian place. We met Enrique there and he was alone this time. He ordered a carafe of local white wine, and we ordered dishes that he recommended. Everything was superb of course. Enrique then said, "tomorrow morning we will go to the hall for you to rehearse and after that I would like to take you out to the countryside so you can see some of Columbia." I asked "is there any danger in going there? I know gangs roam some of the streets and we don't want to be exposed unnecessarily." Enrique assured me we would not be taken anywhere that he didn't think was safe and we would have our two escorts along to make sure. I asked Eve if she was okay with it and she said, "I trust Enrique will have our backs and it would be nice to see some of the countryside." So that was the plan for tomorrow. Hopefully all would go as planned.

The next morning, we had breakfast in our room and then met Enrique downstairs to go to the hall. In the meantime, Jeanine called back and said she was told there is no rotation, only the two escorts and wasn't sure who the other man was. She told me to keep her informed if we see him in Bogota. She could always send backup to check him out. We said we would let her know if he pops up again. We got into the limo and off we went to the hall and then to see Columbia. It was a beautiful day weather wise so a nice time to get out.

I stepped onto the stage at Lourdes Music Hall and sat down to play a bit. The acoustics weren't as good as in Caracas but I had to make it work. I asked if my chair could be positioned further back so the sound of my notes would reverberate off the back walls. Eve said that was a significant improvement so I made note of where the chair should be. After we were off in the limo, I asked Enrique if I could have a whiskey from the limo bar and he gladly obliged of course.

As we drove out of the city into the countryside, we could see some of the gentrification lines of the city. From an area of affluence and wealth to shacks and poverty. There seemed to be no middle class in Columbia. After about a half hour outside the city, we were taken to a beautiful small town square. It seemed every town had a church and town square and of course, the local café. We sat down for a cup of fabulous Columbian coffee when I noticed that same man out in the square not far from our limo. I elbowed Eve and she saw him too. Now this could not have been a coincidence any longer and we tried to point him out to Enrique but when he went to look the man was gone. This was alarming so we asked Enrique if we could go back to the hotel asap. We just would feel more comfortable there. He answered "of course, I don't want either of you to worry for your safety so we will head back immediately."

The recital at Lourdes Music Hall came and I stepped out onto the stage confident it would go well. Unfortunately, seeing the man following us again in Bogota didn't help as the thought sat in the back of my mind always. My performance went fairly well without any major hitches as I felt I was becoming more comfortable with the program and the audience was very receptive. I did my Lauro encore and was offstage quickly after that. Eve and I went back to the hotel to prepare for our trip to Lima, Peru the next morning. Carmen had called to confirm the pickup time, we were glad to be getting out of Columbia. Who knew what would await us in Peru.

CHAPTER 6

Lima

We left Bogota in our private charter jet and Carmen was of course a great hostess. The flight was a short one again, but we were treated to some great tapas on the plane and a great view of the Andes Mountains. Once landing in Lima, Peru we were picked up by a large black SUV and driven to the Jose Antonio Executive Hotel just outside the center of the city. The hotel wasn't far from the beautiful cliffs of the Pacific Ocean a couple of blocks away, so we were excited to see Lima a bit but also very wary about our movements.

Eve and I settled in at the hotel and would again dine there later. My recital in Lima would be at the Gran Teatro Nacional del Perú on May 17th, another older beautiful hall with supposedly great acoustics. In two days, I would have my rehearsal at the hall. We wanted to get out and walk over to the shopping area that is built on the edge of the cliffs and maybe have a drink there but wanted to check in with Enrique first. Our security escorts had come along on the flight over and would watch over us. The area seemed very safe, but we weren't sure if our friend would show up again.

Enrique was staying in the hotel also and we called his room and told him what we wanted to do. He said he would love to accompany us over there, so we made plans to go over for a late lunch around 2pm. On our walk over to the cliffs we perused the area and saw no reason to be concerned. The views from the walkway of the cliffs and ocean were staggering, incredibly beautiful! Carmen joined us for lunch, I wasn't sure if she was staying with Enrique but surmised, she was, and we enjoyed pisco sours, the native drink made of brandy and passionfruit. From there we ordered oysters, octopus and other dishes and shared them. Enrique wanted us to experience some of the cuisine of Peru.

On our walk back to the hotel I pulled Enrique aside and asked him if he had heard anything from our escorts or Jeanine about the man that had been following us. He said, "no not yet, but I will follow up today." I asked him "are Americans at risk here or in South America in general?" He answered "not in Peru for sure but more so in Columbia and Venezuela where the gangs are more active. Brazil and Argentina have not had many incidents of violence involving Americans that I know of. They thrive on the tourism, so the government keeps that in check, I'm sure." I felt somewhat reassured for the rest of our trip.

Once arriving back at the hotel, I practiced for an hour and then we took a short nap that turned into a love making session again which then turned into a nap, not sure how that happens sometimes but I'll take it. Eve said tomorrow she wanted to do some shopping so we would head out early into the center of town that was bustling with activity.

Day of rehearsal came and as I stepped out onto the stage of the Gran Teatro Nacional del Perú, I noticed how aesthetically pleasing it was. The balcony was very ornate, and the seats were a comfortable maroon color. I was sure many great artists had performed here. The acoustics were perfect, as I was told by Eve, and lived up to the hall's reputation. I played for about an hour and really enjoyed the ambience. I was sure the recital would go great.

Recital day came and I was ready to kill it. Again, the hall was about three quarters full, so I considered the turnout to be pretty good. Right from the start I was flying, my hands felt like they had taken over and the guitar was just an extension of my body. I performed the Suite Venezolana and Mozart Variations to perfection and the Walton Bagatelles with relative ease and fluency. As I played my encore, I was saying to myself, "this is damn good." Of course, that kind of overconfidence can get a performer into trouble, but not tonight it seemed.

We were to leave Peru the following morning for Rio de Janeiro, Brazil, as I was reminded by Carmen, so just enjoyed a drink back at the hotel to rest up for the trip tomorrow that would be longer than usual. Brazil is a huge country with Rio being on the eastern coast so in essence, we were flying from one side of the continent over the Andes Mountains to the other side. From the Pacific Ocean to the South Atlantic Ocean. It would take a few hours, so I planned to relax and settle in on the plane.

We boarded the plane around 10am and Carmen came up to Eve and I asking if we needed anything to make our trip more comfortable. The bottle of McCallum 12 was already in my seat so I just answered "I'm good, Eve you?" She just responded "I have you near so I couldn't be better" as she hugged my arm. We would be landing in Rio at a private airport later in the day, so I just kicked back and relaxed feeling good about my performance. The thought of the small, dark skinned, muscular man didn't enter my mind. Although I knew it would reappear at some point.

CHAPTER 7

Rio de Janeiro

As we descended into Rio as it was known to the locals, I saw the famous *Christ the Redeemer* statue that overlooks the city. With the city, ocean, and mountains surrounding it was an awesome sight. Rio had the reputation of being a party city, so we were looking forward to seeing what it was really like. The van picked us up at the airport and we drove into the heart of the city and close to the water to Hotel Nacional Rio De Janeiro. It was right by the ocean and our room had a fabulous view. Eve and I got settled in; my recital would be on May 24th at the Municipal Theater of Rio de Janeiro. The hall had another great reputation for its acoustics, and I was looking forward to getting in there to try it out.

Again, we chose to dine in the hotel, the flight had been a long one and we wanted to recover a bit. By the time we got to our room it was almost time for dinner. That is, if you are American, it was almost time for dinner. Most Cariocas, as most Brazilians from Rio are known, eat dinner at 9pm or after like many European countries. That was something I don't think I would ever get used to. The hotel restaurant was empty since it was early for them, so we sat to eat and ordered caipirinhas, the national fruity drink of Brazil. We were in a Portuguese speaking country now not Spanish, so the culture was different and interesting for sure. After dinner drinks, we went up to rest and expected a call from Enrique about our itinerary here in Rio.

Sure enough the call came right at 8pm. Enrique was always prompt and when he said he would call, that was guaranteed and comforting to us. He said we had a day to kill before going to the hall for a rehearsal so he would pick us up at 10am and we could tour Rio. It sounded like a fun day, so we went to bed looking forward to the next day's adventure.

We met in the lobby of the hotel in the morning and were off around town. Rio de Janeiro is a very diverse city with many different kinds of neighborhoods. Having been colonized by the Portuguese in 1500, it had gone through many shifts in culture including the large influx of Europeans in the twentieth century. Enrique took us to a typical Brazilian restaurant, and we ate like royalty for basically nothing in terms of money. Then we visited many of the cultural monuments and museums of the city. Eve and I were certainly getting an education on the different South American countries. Each culture was different and especially Brazilian!

When we got back to the hotel, we decided to go around the corner to a small restaurant that the concierge had recommended to us. We made sure our escorts were with us when we went since Enrique wasn't with us. Once there we were seated and of course ordered caipirinhas. I looked across the room and elbowed Eve about who was sitting at a table in the corner. It was guess who, the man who was following us. I asked her, "do you want to leave and go back to the hotel?" Eve just said, "hell no, I won't let this man interfere with our trip." I wasn't sure if that was the best thing to do but didn't argue with her. We ate and headed back to the hotel when we heard but didn't see a scuffle behind us. Upon hearing something going on back there we rushed back to the hotel. We were both spooked by it and ran like hell.

The next morning Jeanine called and said "one of our escorts has gotten into an altercation with a man who fit the description you supplied. Apparently, he was coming out of the restaurant following us and was jumped by this man and knocked out cold. He is in a hospital in Rio but is okay and will recover fine. For the remainder of your stay in Rio I suggest you stay in the hotel where we can protect you until we can get a replacement for him." We agreed of course since in two days I would have my recital in Rio and we would be off to Buenos Aires the next day.

Recital day came and I stepped out onstage at the Municipal Theater of Rio de Janeiro. I was determined to play my best and not let the circumstances interfere with the tour. Again, as I had experienced before, it was as if my hands and brain took over and I was just a spectator watching myself perform. It is an amazing experience when this happens and had happened before to me on the last tour as well, so I just took it in. It was a very ethereal experience and after it was over I was a bit numb with no explanation of what had just happened. Eve, Enrique, and Carmen once again joined me backstage and congratulated me on an exceptional performance. Enrique said "of all the performances you have done on this tour that was by far the best, everything just flowed in your hands." I thanked him for the comments, and we headed back to the hotel to get ready to depart in the morning. I was looking forward to getting the tour over with and heading back to New York City. As I was to find out, that would be a real task.

CHAPTER 8

Buenos Aires

As we headed into Buenos Aires, Argentina, I reflected on what had just happened. Or at least what I thought might be going on. We were obviously being followed but why? Could it be related to what happened in Europe or was it something else. I knew that Jeanine was on a plane from the states on her way to Buenos Aires. I was hoping she had some further information for us and would find out later. The flight took a few hours, so we got to chill a bit in the plane. Once we landed, we were picked up and taken to Hotel Buenos Aires in the heart of the city. I would be performing on June 1st at the Teatro Colón, another breathtaking concert hall, as I was told.

We settled in at the hotel, Jeanine wasn't expected to arrive until the evening and would be staying at our hotel. Enrique and Carmen were going to meet us for dinner at our hotel since it was our first night there. They were staying in another hotel since Carmen had family in Buenos Aires and wanted to be nearer to them. I was happy we had made it to the last leg of our trip and sat down to practice for an hour while Eve went to the gift shop in the hotel. I asked her to please not leave the hotel, and she agreed that was the wisest thing to do. We were down to one escort until they could replace the other that was attacked. Eve sent a get well note to him thanking him for his being there to protect us. After practicing for an hour, I texted Eve to meet me and went down to the hotel bar for you know what, McCallum 12 as a pre-dinner drink. Eve showed up and ordered a prosecco. She showed me what she had bought for her assistant and Andrew Sisley back in New York as thanks for watching the forts for us. Eve asked "any idea what Jeanine will say when she gets in later? She must have some more information on what is going on." I just answered, "I have no idea, but I know she has our backs." Eve just joked "I know she has your back; I've known she has a crush on you for years." I said laughingly "well I guess that's a good thing since she will try harder to protect us." Eve just gave me one of her patented looks, I had seen that before.

Enrique showed up with Carmen who of course looked fabulously sexy. I thought "why shouldn't I have a Latin beauty to accompany me around on the tour, after all I am now a world-renowned artist." I could imagine what Eve was thinking. More like "who are you kidding Jonathan, stop fantasizing." Anyway, we proceeded to order dishes. Argentina being known for their grilled meats called parrillada, and wine was exactly what we had for dinner. Incredible steaks and Malbec wines from Mendoza, the main wine growing region in Argentina. Dessert was of course their dulce de leche so famous in Argentina. I said to Enrique, "I would love to get out to some vineyards in Mendoza if we can." He replied "well it is a way from here, but I'll see what we can arrange. It might be a great way to end the tour. I'll let you know." We had after dinner drinks and said our goodbyes and headed up to the room. Once we got there the phone rang, it was Jeanine. I picked up and she said, "we should meet downstairs, I have some intel for you about what possibly might be going on although it's not confirmed, just speculation at this point." I said of course and we planned to meet downstairs in the lobby at 10:30pm.

When Eve and I got downstairs we met Jeanine and went to the far corner of the lobby that was unoccupied. Jeanine seemed a bit disheveled but that may have been because she just got off a long plane ride from New York. She started by telling us the Agency had picked up on increased drug gang activity here in Buenos Aires and that the word was out that Americans might be at risk. Eve followed "do you consider us to be at risk here because if so, we will just cancel the recital here and head back to the states?" Jeanine responded, "we think the risk here for you is minimal, but the decision would be yours if you want to do that." I chimed in "we will have to discuss it; I would hate to do that since it could have major repercussions on my career." Eve just said she was on the fence about it, and we would have to discuss it tonight. I agreed that was a good way to go. The recital was in four days so I felt if we could hold out until afterwards, we'd be home free. Jeanine said, "let's speak in the morning, I need to get some rest so you both should sleep on it, and we will go from there." We thanked her and I asked Eve if she was up for a nightcap at the bar to discuss it and she said, "sure why not."

We sat at a far corner table at the bar and looked at each other, both of us wondering if we should take the chance and stay to finish out the tour? She opened "Jonathan, I think we should stay and finish it out. You've worked so hard for this and should reap the benefits of it. Running away would be the worst thing to do I think." I countered "but if something happened to you, I would never forgive myself, it may just be too dangerous to stay, after all, we are being followed for a reason." She went on "there comes a time when we have to make a decision that might be risky but doing the cowardly thing is not the answer." I said, "if you really think we should stay then I will finish out the tour with a bang, we have to be smart and stay in the hotel for the most part then." Eve agreed, Jeanine had posted another escort in the hotel, so we were back to two and felt safer.

The following day we went to the Teatro Colón so I could test out the hall and position my chair and footstool. Once again, the acoustics were fantastic, it was very interesting to me how many great concert halls there are in South America, and I've performed now in a few of them. I played for about an hour, and we headed out for lunch with our entourage and then back to the hotel. Enrique, Carmen, Jeanine, Eve and I were to have dinner in the hotel at 8pm. I thought this would be a good opportunity to discuss some details of the tour. We went down to the bar early to have a drink and chill a bit. Both of us were feeling a bit tense.

Everyone showed up on time and we chose a table in an isolated part of the restaurant. Once we were seated Jeanine spoke to all of us saying there has been considerable chatter online about the drug cartels and their intensions of grabbing Americans as bargaining chips to get some of their own people released. She went on "it is unclear about the specifics such as who, when, and where so we will just have to be very vigilant and aware of our surroundings." We told Jeanine that we were staying and intended to finish the tour, I didn't come this far to run away." She responded "I admire your chutzpah and will help to keep you both safe as much as possible." Enrique and Carmen agreed as well to help where they could. We finished dinner, the next day was the recital at Teatro Colon, so I wanted to practice a bit before hitting the sack early. And I wanted to be ready for anything that might happen.

CHAPTER 9

The Recital

The next morning, we got up, had a late breakfast in the room and just chilled until the time we had to leave for the hall. I could tell Eve was unsettled by the whole thing, but she is a trooper and pretty much ready for anything. We left for the hall that was about twenty minutes away at 4:30pm. I wanted to get there a bit early to warm up and get settled. Eve whipped out a flask in the dressing room with a shot of McCallum 12, she knew that calmed me down as long as I didn't have too much, I am fine.

I stepped out onto the stage trying to focus and not think about any of our discussions. I dove into the Renaissance pieces with a fervor and then flew through the first half of the program. I think my tempos were a bit fast probably from nerves, but my technique was clean. The audience was very receptive, and the hall looked sold out, probably from all the advanced promotion they had done.

When I came offstage at intermission Enrique came running up to me shouting, "Jonathan, Eve is missing. We can't find her anywhere! Carmen is gone too?" I asked him, "did you check my dressing room?" He said, "yes of course, everywhere, the bathrooms and lobby too, I informed Jeanine and she is on it, they are checking the hall's camera footage to see if anything shows up." I asked Enrique where Jeanine was, and he said in the security room of the hall with the guards.

I headed over there and they let me in to see her. Jeanine said, "we are checking all possibilities, I will let you know when we find something." I was a mess; it was time for me to go out for the second half. I asked Jeanine "should I cancel the second half?" She just responded, "since we are unsure where Eve is it makes no sense to cancel at this point, I'm sure I will have some information for you when you finish." I agreed and said I'll do the best I can.

I went out for the second half to play but was missing a big part of me. If it's bad news my head will explode, so I thought. My performance in the second half was listless and uninspired, and rightfully so. I couldn't wait to get off stage! When I finally did Jeanine was in my dressing room. She said we need to talk but not here. Let's go to Agency headquarters here in Buenos Aires, they have all the information and resources. We hopped in the black sedan and headed there not knowing what to expect. I was hoping for the best of course.

CHAPTER 10

The Disappearance

We arrived at Agency headquarters and were ushered upstairs to a conference room. The head of the Agency there was Lionel Delgado who was originally from Columbia and recruited and trained by the CIA because of his military background fighting the drug cartels in Bogota. Enrique was there as well but where was Carmen? We sat down and Lionel started right in "Jonathan, security footage shows your wife was absconded and put into a blue sedan. Enrique here identified the short muscular man who had been following you was with her. The same man that you had let Jeanine know about. Another bit of information was Carmen Roldan was with them. Apparently, she was part of the plot to kidnap Eve." I asked "what could they possibly want with her? Can I see the footage?" Lionel replied, "yes of course, she is American and the cartels use Americans as pawns to get their own people released from prison." I asked, "do you have any idea where she is now?" Lionel replied "probably on her way to the hills of Bogota, that is where they keep all their hostages. We have an idea where they are but it's hard to pinpoint since it is in the jungle areas of Columbia. As soon as we have more intel on this, we will inform you. I suggest for now you stay calm and work with us to get your wife back." I replied of course, what else can I do at this point.

I was led into a room with video screens with Jeanine and Lionel. Lionel said, "we will run the footage for you, but it will probably be a bit alarming, your wife didn't go willingly." As they ran the footage Eve was pushed into the sedan by Carmen and the other assailant. She fought with them but to no avail. I could see blood on her face. The guess is that she was grabbed when she went to the lady's room and forced out a window there. Now I was worried, I knew Eve and that she could be a tough person when confronted. I just hoped she used restraint knowing her fighting them at this point is a losing battle.

Jeanine suggested we go back to the hotel to strategize with Enrique. We met at the bar at a secluded table. Enrique came too. He said "I'm in shock, I had no idea Carmen was working with the cartels. She was very good, there were no clues, including all the time I spent in bed with her. She is good, very good at deceiving, a great actress!" I asked Jeanine what she thought was happening. She said, "I'm sure Lionel is working all the angles, he is very good at what he does and a bulldog in tracking these people down." I said, "I'm happy to hear that and that he is on the case." Jeanine said "Jonathan, is there anything I can do for you that will ease your anxiety in any way?" I said "yes, get my wife back to me safe." She said she admired my commitment and love for her and will do all in her power to honor my wish. She also went on, "Jonathan, be ready to leave for Columbia at any point, I think we are all headed there momentarily." I said I'm ready any time and headed back to my room to pack all our stuff. Jeanine said she would take care of our belongings wherever we go. I was glad she was here; I needed someone to calm me down and she knew how.

CHAPTER 11

In Pursuit

Early the next morning we flew out to Bogota. The Agency traced Eve's route to a private airport with the plane heading to Bogota. My greatest fears had happened. Eve could disappear and not be heard from for years. Apparently, the gang that had kidnapped her was the Esteves Cartel headed by Geno Esteves, a notorious drug lord and criminal. The Esteves Cartel had their hands in everything and even politicians in their back pockets. Lionel joined us on the plane and said "Jonathan, I want you to know, I will follow this through until we have Eve back safely, you have my word on that." I thanked him and said anyway I could help; I would be up for it. After my experience in Europe, I was up for anything. Just give me a gun and I'll do what I must. Of course, the Agency was not about to do that at this point due to my lack of experience. But I think I held my own in Europe and would do so here as well.

We were put up in a safehouse in Bogota just to be cautious. The safehouse was guarded twenty-four hours a day. I told Jeanine to make sure Lionel includes me in on any briefings regarding Eve. She said she would try but some things were classified, and I couldn't be there. I said I understood but didn't want to be excluded from any updates on Eve. She agreed and we settled in at the safehouse waiting for any information on where Eve might be. It was nerve racking.

The next morning, we were ushered into what looked like a situation room. We met with Colonel Sanchez of the Columbian Military Drug Enforcement Unit and Lionel from the Agency. Colonel Sanchez was charged with tracking down the Esteves Group as they were known. He went on to say in broken English "we have an idea where your wife is being held but haven't pinpointed the exact location yet. The Esteves Group is known to take hostages into the jungle not far from Bogota. They have not communicated anything yet about their demands so the whole scenario will unfold soon, I'm sure. Once we know something more definite, we will inform you. Please be patient Mr. Lanbourne, I'm sure we will hear from them soon." I thanked the Colonel and Lionel and said "of course, I hope you will have some intel soon on this, time is of the essence." They both assured me they knew that, every minute counts.

Upon returning to the safehouse we settled in, waiting to hear. Jeanine asked if I needed anything, I answered "McCallum 12 por favor!" She said, of course, and the bottle arrived. It must have been two in the morning when the phone rang. It was Lionel "we have intelligence on where Eve is, a car will take you back to headquarters in fifteen minutes. Please be ready downstairs." I said "of course!"

We arrived back at the situation room and were quickly briefed. The Colonel went on "we received a request to exchange your wife for a notorious drug kingpin, Jose Antonio Alvarez, who has been in jail now for five years. We are hoping we can pinpoint where your wife is before we must make a decision on this. The demand says we have forty-eight hours otherwise they will execute her. I asked for proof of life, and they responded by saying we will contact you later by video. Jonathan, please understand this is something they say all the time in their requests. It's part of the way they do business. We somehow always manage to get around this in our negotiations. We will update you soon again so hang tight and be patient, that is the way these things work. When they let us know when the video feed will be live, we will get you back here and hopefully you can speak with Eve to confirm she is okay."

I went back to the safehouse with Jeanine and Lionel again and we had lunch there, whatever I could get down. My stomach was churning. Colonel Sanchez was not allowing us to leave unescorted, so we had to hunker down and wait for any news. That didn't take long, we were informed the video feed would happen at 4pm today. We were all headed back to the situation room as I hoped for the best.

We sat down at the roundtable where I'm sure this was a common occurrence, you could see Colonel Sanchez had done this hundreds of times, hopefully with success. We were joined by a representative from the United States Embassy in Bogota who introduced himself as Lawrence Sumfield. He went on to say "since your wife is an American citizen I need to monitor the negotiations." I replied, "the more help we can get the better."

The video feed came up and I could see a man whose face was covered and also see Eve in the background. The man's voice was distorted as well, he said in Spanish, "here is your proof of life," as the camera zoomed in on Eve. I could see her blouse was torn and there was blood on it and her face. She looked terrified but was trying to cover it up. The Colonel went on to ask if I could say a few words to her saying it in English to me as well. The man replied, "we will give you one minute to speak and if anything is said regarding any specifics, we will cut you off." The Colonel went on "Jonathan, you have one minute to speak to Eve." I dove in "honey, are you okay? Have they hurt you in any way?" She replied, "except for when they took me I haven't been touched yet, just roughed up a bit." I went on "we are doing everything possible to get you out, please hang in there." Just as I was about to tell her I loved her we were cutoff and the man came back on "you have your proof of life and forty hours left to do the exchange, we expect to hear from you, or you know what will happen. We will be in touch. Keep this video feed open and monitored." All this was translated to me and Jeanine by Lawrence who spoke fluent Spanish.

Later in the same evening we received a call from Colonel Sanchez, he said "we have an informer implanted into the Esteves Group. I've informed the Agency that we received intel from them as to the exact location Eve is being held at. If we can mobilize fast enough, we can set up a rescue plan. It's risky for Eve but it looks like it might be our only choice since the Colombian government will not give up Jose Antonio Alverez in exchange for Eve. They say it is too much to give." I asked the Colonel "what is your assessment of our chances with a rescue attack?" He said he thought the probability was very good that Eve would be rescued but couldn't guarantee it. I said to him "I have to go if the plan is launched, I have to be there, hell or high water." The Colonel said he would try and get permission for me to be there, but I would have to guarantee that I wouldn't interfere with the operation since civilians aren't alowed on these raids. I said "of course, this isn't my first rodeo you know." The Colonel just looked at me and smiled saying "I will do my best to get you approved."

CHAPTER 12

The Plan

The next morning, with less than twenty-four hours to go, Colonel Sanchez confirmed that they had the exact location and were putting together a plan. He asked us to get over to the situation room asap to discuss how it would go down. Jeanine and I dashed out the door, Lionel would meet us over there so we could discuss it amongst ourselves as well.

There were a dozen or so military personnel in the room with me, Jeanine, Lionel and Lawrence. Colonel Sanchez went on to say "we have located the exact location the Esteves Group is holding the hostage. For us to pull off a rescue we must make them believe that the exchange is going to take place. The optimal place to catch them when they are most vulnerable is on their way to the exchange. We received a message from our informant that they will be back up on a video feed in thirty minutes wanting to know if the exchange has been arranged. We of course will tell them it has and request a meeting place amenable to both sides. We will just have to take it from there. Once they board their vehicles and head out, we will launch a raid with two of our anti-drug units. That is where we stand right now. We will reconvene after the video call." The Colonel pulled me aside and said "Jonathan, you only will ride with me and be stationed at a secure location away from the attack. It's best you stay out of harm's way. Pedro and Miguel from the unit will ride with us for protection." I just nodded my affirmation.

Sure enough the hooded man from the Esteves Group showed up on the video call. It went as planned and the exchange was to happen at 8pm tonight in the town square of a small town outside of Bogota named San Miguel. The whole thing was nerve racking, and I was terrified, but I knew I had to keep my head clear and ready for anything. I would use my instincts to determine any move I would make. I wasn't just going to sit back and leave it in the hands of the Colombian military even though I had little choice at this point.

We headed out at 7pm. The raid was supposed to happen at a designated spot along the route just outside of San Miguel. The spot was remote and sparsely populated to prevent any deaths or injuries to civilians. We positioned ourselves about one hundred meters from the route, the Esteves Group's entourage would be passing in about thirty minutes. I was mentally preparing myself for anything and to jump into action if necessary to save my Eve. If anything happened to her, I could never forgive myself. The waiting around was agonizing. Thirty minutes seemed like an eternity.

As we watched the Esteves entourage approach we could see there were six vehicles, four jeep pickup trucks and two black sedans. I figured Eve was in one of the sedans and the others were just Esteves fighters ready to fight. The Colonel would be giving the attack signal any moment. My intuition told me there was something not right about the two sedans. It concerned me that there were two, one could be a decoy. Before the Colonel could give the signal, we heard gunfire around where the anti-drug units were stationed. The Colonel was corresponding with one of the anti-drug unit heads when it went dead. What was going on here? The Colonel said "Jonathan, we have to leave, something has gone wrong, and we need to get out of here." I answered, "I'm not leaving, Eve is in one of those cars and I'm going to find her." The Colonel gave the order to Pedro to head out back to headquarters and just as Pedro nodded, I opened the door and jumped out. I was going to find out what sedan Eve was in and find a way to free her. I had no idea what I was doing but my instincts for things have always been good. The Colonel turned the car around and headed back towards me as I ran towards the Esteves entourage. When they saw they wouldn't reach me in time they turned around and headed back from where they came. As I approached, I noticed one of the pickup trucks they had come in was empty in the back. I guesstimated if I ran like hell I could get in the back and stay hidden. I did just that and luck was on my side, I made it into the back of the truck. The driver and other gunman didn't notice me in the back as much as I could tell. I thought, "well maybe now they will have two hostages" but hoped I could figure out a way to rescue Eve. I could see the Colonel's jeep had stopped and headed back. From what I could surmise the anti-drug unit had been attacked from the rear of their location. The Esteves Group had figured out it was a trap. I could make out more gunfire as I was in the back of the truck not sure where it was coming from and what the result was?

As we approached the encampment in the jungles of Columbia I could see the two black sedans. The truck I was in was the last one of the entourages, so I was unnoticed from behind. I could see them pull up to a large tent and drag Eve out of the car into the tent. I snuck out of the truck once it stopped and into a wooded area not far from it so I wouldn't be noticed. I had to come up with my own plan and had one shot at it or we were all dead. I reached deep into the recesses of my mind and then heard a voice calling "Jonathan, over here!" Who was it calling me?

CHAPTER 13

The Confrontation

I turned to look, and it was Carmen. She must have been the informant in the Esteves Group as far as I could tell. She waved me over, I thought I had no choice but to go with it, whatever the consequences. I ran to her, and she grabbed me by the arm and led me into a small tent where there was another man. She said "you are crazy to come here, things have gone south and I'm sure the Colonel is going to launch a full scale attack any minute. Okay mi amour look, we are going to have to work fast and smart. Pablo here is on our side and will help us to formulate a plan to get Eve away safely. You are going to just have to trust us and do what we say. Understood?" I said "completely!".

Pablo looked at me and said, "have you ever fired a gun?" I said, "yes I've had experience." Of course, I knew it was as an amateur but I wasn't going to tell him that. He said "we need to move fast since we don't know what Geno Esteves will do now. He may harm or kill Eve because he was double crossed by the Colonel. We will move out in ten minutes and encircle the tent where she is. We must take out the two lookouts first. I have another hired gun, Jorge, who will join us, he and I will take out the lookouts once Carmen reports back to us, and then if we have to go in guns a blazing then that might be our only option. Carmen will do intel to let us know the situation in the tent Eve is in. Be prepared, it might go down that way quickly. Load up and get ready." I saw Carmen in the corner of the tent putting on battle gear. She looked like one of those comic book vixens, sexy and loaded, ready to kill. I thought for a second, "how did I get here again?"

We moved out of the tent one by one and spread out in different directions taking cover wherever we could. Since they knew Carmen, she would go into the tent where Eve was and scout it out. Since she was gorgeous, she could get away with a lot and knew it. I saw Carmen flirt with one of the lookouts and then enter the tent. We waited for her to come out with a report so we could move. Pablo had given me an earpiece so we all could communicate when the time came. Sure enough, Carmen came out and walked away from the tent, over the earpiece she said "Eve is there and has been roughed up a bit but is alive, I saw no sign of Geno. There are two lookouts and two more in the tent. I suggest waiting until we see him enter the tent so we can grab Eve and Geno as well." Pablo went on "I fully agree, let's continue to stake this out. If Geno doesn't come back in fifteen minutes, I say we go in since the Colonel will most certainly be launching an attack, we don't want to wait too long." Carmen replied "agreed."

Fifteen minutes went by and no Geno, Pablo said "spread the word, we are going in in five minutes, Jorge and I will take out the lookouts, after that Carmen and Jonathan will join us for the assault, be ready, I will give the word." Carmen came over to me "Jonathan are you okay with this, you don't have to go in if you don't want to." I replied, "I wouldn't miss this for the world, if something bad happens then so be it, at least I can say I tried, if we live through this." Carmen replied, "I fully understand Jonathan, you must really love her." I just said, "she is my soulmate, what else can I do?"

Pablo came over the earpiece and I could see movement by the tent "Geno has arrived with two more armed guards; our only advantage is we surprise them. Jorge and I will move out to take out the lookouts. Once you see that move in fast, no hesitation, we need to take both Geno and Eve alive!" I could see Pablo and Jorge move out fast taking cover as they got closer to the tent. This was surrealistic to me, how did I get here, it was like a movie I was put in.

As I waited for Pablo's command my stomach was churning, I tried to contain myself and not throw up. I needed to summon up all my strength to save Eve, that thought is what kept me going. I heard Pablo's voice and thought to myself, "here it goes, I'm going to die in Columbia!" "Move out fast and surround the tent, we have disarmed the lookouts, on my order enter the tent and fire first if you see a gun pointed at you, don't wait!" At that moment I got up and ran to the perimeter of the tent awaiting Pablo's command. Just as I got there, I could hear gunshots coming from outside of the encampment. Pablo came on again "it's the Colonel, they have launched an attack, we need to stay put to see how this unfolds, stay in your place."

I thought to myself "how long can we wait; they might harm or kill Eve?" I got up and burst into the tent with my gun ready to shoot. As I entered, I saw two guards and Geno watching over Eve. Geno was powerfully built with a cropped CIA style haircut. We all froze in place, Geno said "you must be the husband, I was saving this final torture for your eyes only so I'm glad you are here. How would you like me to kill your wife, your choice. Gunshot to the head? Cut her throat? Strangle her? At this point I have nothing to lose. They will catch me and send me to jail, and I will be out in a few months regardless of what I do here, so tell me, what do you prefer since it will be the last time you see her alive?" I could see Eve tied up, bloody and in pain from whatever they had done to her. I needed to buy some time "Geno, how does killing her help you? We have nothing to do with the government here." Geno answered "the Colonel double crossed me by not ever meaning to do the exchange. This will show him what happens when you double cross the Esteves Group."

Just as Geno finished speaking a large blast hit the corner of the tent. We were all thrown through the air and I landed somewhere near where Eve was. I looked around and apparently everyone in the tent was discombobulated and disoriented. I thought fast and got up and ran towards Eve, she was on the ground but seemed okay. I untied her and said, "we need to get out of here, run like hell!" We dashed towards the tent door as I shielded Eve, just then I heard a gunshot and felt extreme pain in my left arm. I was hit as we tried to get out of the tent. I wasn't sure where Geno was and who fired it but knew we had to keep moving if we were to survive.

We exited the tent and were met by Pablo and Carmen, Carmen said "move fast, we need to find cover since the Colonel's anti-drug units are moving in fast." We ran into the jungle and hunkered down behind a group of trees. Eve looked at me, "you are injured, we need to get pressure on that wound asap, Carmen, do you have anything we can use to tie a tourniquet on his arm?" Carmen then tore off part of her shirt and gave it to Eve saying, "use this, just tie it tight enough to stop the bleeding." My Eve did just that. I looked at Carmen and she basically was shirtless. I thought how gorgeous she was. What a time to have those thoughts. My arm seemed to hurt less suddenly; Eve was there holding my hand.

Pablo came over the earpiece, "where is your location? You went in alone Jonathan, that wasn't advisable. We saw you run out with Eve but lost you in the smoke. Let us know where you are so we can extract you." Carmen went on to provide him with our exact location since she was familiar with the camp. She then turned to me "you are very brave Jonathan, I hope I find a man who is as devoted to me as you are to Eve. Now it is time to get you both out of here asap." I just responded, "I really didn't think, I just reacted, I guess that is a good thing." Carmen nodded.

When the smoke cleared from the explosion, I could see the tent and men running out of it. One looked like Geno. I said to Carmen "that looks like Geno Esteves, are you going to apprehend him?" She said her priority now was getting us out of here and would leave that up to the Colonel and his forces. I said I appreciate that, but he needs to answer for what he has done to Eve. Carmen just replied, "he will, we will make sure of that, I have been working him and his group for two years now. I know how to get to them." I just replied, "I hope so!"

Pablo and Jorge showed up next to us in a matter of minutes. Just then the Colonel's forces were attacking, and bullets were flying everywhere. Pablo said, "wait for my signal and then move fast!" About thirty seconds later Pablo said, "move out!" We followed him and Jorge into the jungle and eventually to a road that led down to a ravine. Eve asked, "Jon are you okay, don't pass out on us please!" I said, "I'm fine, let's keep pushing ahead." We got down to the bottom of the ravine and there were two boats there to take us down the river and out of immediate danger. We hopped in and were in for a bumpy ride. I thought "I'm feeling woozy," and then the lights went out as I lost consciousness.

CHAPTER 14

The Aftermath

The next thing I remember is waking up in a hospital bed after I was given blood transfusions apparently. Eve was there watching me; she had bandages over where she had been injured on her face and arms. I asked, "are we okay?" She answered "we are my love; you need to heal and then we are back to the states. The Agency wants to debrief us before we leave. You will be in here for another day." I asked, "what happened to Geno, did they catch him?" She said she wasn't sure and just said, "get some rest, you need to heal, and we can go from there." Eve always knew how to take charge in tough situations, and it was amazing she came through this okay, I hoped. Who knew what the current and future mental toll will be on both of us?

Two days later we were escorted over to Agency head-quarters by Jeanine, Lionel, and two other agents, Jeanine said, "I can't believe something like this happened to you again Jon, you must attract trouble when you go on tour.

I'm just so glad you and Eve came through this okay." We sat down at a round table with Lionel and an agent named Alessandro, who was in charge in Bogota. As we recounted how everything went down, I asked "what happened to Geno Esteves? Was he caught?" Alessandro went on to say "unfortunately, he got away but Colonel Sanchez has a lead on where he is headed so hopefully, he will be apprehended soon. It's not easy to catch these drug lords here, they know how to avoid that in very shrewd ways." I asked again "are we in danger since he is still out there and wants revenge for being double crossed?" His reply was "the Agency does not feel you or your wife are in any danger anymore. Geno will try and seek his revenge in other ways. You both don't mean much to him anymore at this point we feel." I just answered, "I hope that is the case!"

We headed back to the safehouse to pick up our luggage and then to the airport. Jeanine told us she would see us in New York. It was time to get the hell out of South America asap. Eve and I were both like zombies in the car and ready for the long trip home. We were escorted to the plane by two agents, one of which would be on the flight with us. The State Department back in the US asked to meet with us once we got back. This ordeal seemed like it would never end. I knew we both would need therapy back in New York for PTSD to recover properly. I was also thankful for the painkillers I was given since my arm ached like hell when I wasn't on them.

We were driven to the airport and boarded the flight in first class seating with the Agency's agent next to us. As we ascended to thirty thousand feet, I was never so happy to get out of a country with Eve and I still intact. I thought to myself "no more tours please!" But who knew what the future would bring. I knew it would take us awhile to be ourselves again.

CHAPTER 15

Finally, Home

We landed at JFK airport around 4pm in the afternoon and were helped with our baggage into a limo waiting for us. The Agency had provided it, Eve and I were not in great shape physically or mentally, so our State Department meeting was put off until tomorrow. I said to Eve. "I hope we have a bottle of McCallum at home, pain killers or not I'm having a glass." Eve answered, "me too Jon, then I just want you to hold me, with your good arm of course, I need to be close to you to-night." I just replied "I need that too love, it's been a crazy ride the last few weeks. Somehow, we need to put it behind us at some point and be healthy again." Eve just nodded.

I called the University and spoke with Andrew Sisley who again oversaw the department and told him I got injured on the tour and will put in for some time off to recover. He just told me to let him know when I was coming back. Honestly, the way I felt, I didn't know if I wanted to go back to my old life. My career seemed inconsequential now. Time would tell what the future would be. We went back to the apartment, poured the whiskey and fell into each other's arms falling asleep immediately.

The next morning, we were driven over to the State Department's office in midtown Manhattan. Jeanine joined us as we were seated in a room. Two officials entered the room, a man and woman who introduced themselves as Lawrence Johnson and Kimberly Lassiter, both cultural attaches of South America. Lawrence started off by saying "we were very sorry to hear about your troubles in South America. We are here just to get information from you both just in case this happens to another American citizen. Maybe next time we can prevent it." As we recounted to them the events of the past few weeks my mind went to Geno. Was he apprehended? Or better yet killed? Jeanine had told us she didn't have any further information about him at this point.

When we finished Lawerence and Kimberly gave us their cards and asked us to call them if we had any further details to tell them. I just asked if they had information on Geno Esteves to please let us know. They both agreed they would. Jeanine then asked, "why don't we go for lunch somewhere nearby, I'd like to treat you both." We agreed and off we went. With my arm in a sling, we sat down in a café not far from where we were interviewed. As I looked to the corner of the café there he was, yes it was the man who had kidnapped Eve, now here in New York. I elbowed Eve, look at three o'clock, our friend is back. Jeanine said "just stay put, I'm going to call in a team to apprehend him." Eve said, "I can't believe this, we are never going to be safe."

Jeanine got on her cell phone and within five minutes three Agency agents had entered the café. They were covering up who they were and took a table near the assailant. Jeanine said "here is the plan, we are going to get up and walk out. If he follows our men will grab him. Got it?" We both nodded. As planned, we rose and walked with Jeanine towards the door of the café. As we exited sure enough our South American friend got up and headed towards the door to follow us. The agents then waited for him to get outside and then headed towards him to apprehend him. When he knew he was being followed he started running and went off in a back street with the agents in hot pursuit. Jeanine rushed us into a car that took off for Agency headquarters.

When we arrived, Jeanine had news they had killed the assailant. He had drawn a gun on the agents, and they had no choice but to fire back. They had hoped to catch him to interrogate him regarding the whereabouts of Geno Esteves. But that unfortunately would not be possible now. Once we got to Agency headquarters Jeanine told us she would post another agent for surveillance outside our apartment building and give us an emergency phone number as well for immediate response. It seemed the nightmare would not end, and we had to endure it.

CHAPTER 16

South American Epilogue

The next morning, we received a call from Jeanine, she said she had good news, they had captured Geno Esteves at the airport trying to escape Columbia. We took a breath of relief, and I asked Jeanine "what is our exposure now, are we still in danger?" She answered "we cannot be one hundred percent sure, but it seems you and Eve are out of danger. Geno will go to jail for many years, and we think you both would be a low priority on his list. Let's hope it stays that way." I just replied, "amen to that."

A few days later I was feeling a bit better, and my sling had been removed so I headed over to the university. Andrew was working with a student and I just sat in and watched. It was then I realized how much I missed the guitar and what teaching, practicing, and performing has brought to my life. The South American tour it seemed was a rousing success.

My reviews were great even though because of what was going on I didn't think I performed my best. But the responses were all positive. I was ready to start again, determined, it was time to get back to work!

Eve and I spent a great summer together being closer than ever. I didn't know what adventures lye ahead in our future, but I knew I wanted her along as my partner. We will move forward where anything can happen, and whatever does, will have to be with no strings attached.

Acknowledgements

My thanks go out to many people who helped and donated their time to make this book possible. To Sophia Angelica Nitkin, my daughter, for editing the content ideas and giving basic advice. Her knowledge of music and journalism degree paid off hugely in assisting me. To Alice and Ben Machlin, Alice for the cover design and artwork throughout the book and Ben for editing the structure and grammar. Both of your knowledge in your respective fields are impressive and were invaluable to me. To Christopher Rybin, my adopted stepson, just for being Chris. And to my guitar colleagues, music community, my musical uncle Howard Fraidkin, and long passed teacher, Leonid Bolotine, for having instilled in me the inspiration to write this book. Without my background in classical guitar over the years, I wouldn't have been able to complete this. Lastly, to my better half, Eve Ann Machlin, for the encouragement and love to finish writing this book and give it to the world.

About the Author

Andrew Nitkin has been involved with successful business-
es as an entrepreneur, arts administrator, musician, and
teacher since the 1970's. He founded and ran a music school,
retail shop, artist management and performance space in
New York City for three decades. After selling his business
in New York he went to work at The Wharton Institute for
the Performing Arts in New Jersey as an executive administrator and guitar instructor helping to build it into the larg-
est non-profit educational performing arts organization in
New Jersey.

Upon stepping down from his Director position at
Wharton, Andrew Nitkin decided the best way to share his
life experience in the performing arts, finance, and lifestyle

with others was to author books on the subjects that deal with real life situations both fictional and real. Andrew maintains a music and writing studio in Scotch Plains, New Jersey where he also continues to teach the guitar. **Strings Attached** is his debut book with more projects planned to be released in 2025-26 in both fiction and non-fiction genres. His mission is to add value to people's lives by entertaining them as well as providing valuable lifestyle information for everyday living.